He Lived For Vengeance

Taking desperate risks, Mark Revenue had penetrated the closely guarded hills high above the Rafter T Ranch. Immediately, the renegade LeGrue threw a line of armed guards around the entire area.

But before LeGrue's hardcases closed in, Revenue spotted the evidence he'd come from Texas to find—evidence that his rustled herd of cattle was hidden on Rafter T range.

Now all he had to do was run the grim gauntlet of gunhawks surrounding him. The odds were fifty-to-one against his survival. But the Texan was a man with cold steel in his backbone and hot vengeance in his heart. And when he plunged into action neither one man nor fifty could safely face his roaring Colts.

D0354010

Bestselling **POPULAR LIBRARY** Westerns

25c per copy

TWO ACTION-PACKED NOVELS
OF THE UNTAMED WEST

VENGEANCE TRAIL

ERNEST HAYCOX

AUTHOR OF "RIDERS WEST"
AND "WHISPERING RANGE"

POPULAR LIBRARY
NEW YORK

CONTENTS

ERNEST HAYCOX
WESTERN BOOKS
Published by Popular Library

VENGEANCE
TRAIL

CHAPTER 1

Twelve hundred miles north and west of Texas, Mark Revenue reined his horse before a ranch gate and lifted his gray, level glance to the barrier of sawtooth peaks. Here were the Wyoming mountains at last, casting their very shadow upon him, sending the cold breath of their lonely tops against his face. Here at last were the mountains he had seen from far across the heat-blistered plains, not the same mountains but others, individual masses of that continuous jagged upland he had paralleled in his journey along the flat, beaten, baked Chisholm Trail.

One after another they had kept with Mark Revenue, dim and blue and remote through the prairie haze—Spanish Peak, Sangre de Cristo, Front Range, Medicine Bow, the Laramie. Now, finally, a westering fork of the great cattle trail brought him fair and square into the Wind River country. And in front of a ranch gate that seemed to lie athwart the only visible pass up and across the stark sentinels lying so somber and everlasting in the final emblazoning shafts of the day's sun.

The stiff trail onward did not daunt Mark Revenue. He had traveled too far and with too great an urgency in his heart to be stopped by the prospect of miles tipped on edge. But the gate was a different matter. It was a portent, a symbol. It held a message for him. And, folding his hands on the saddle horn, he thoughtfully considered it.

"Time," said he in a slow soft drawl, "to stop and rest. Time to pause and consider and bend an ear. The trail's petered down to just rabbit tracks in the dust. I've outrun my shadow."

The clang of a bell carried through the still, thin air with a resonant clarity. Mark Revenue nodded his head quietly and pushed his horse against the gate. He lifted the latch bar, passed through and tarried a moment to make sure an attached dead-weight swung the portal shut. Inside this gateway, and enclosed by a high pole fence, were all the accumulated sheds and corrals and buildings of a substantial ranch. The lane he embarked on was like a street. Bunkhouses, blacksmith shop, toolshed and store quarters fronted it; at the far end stood a big house with a generous porch and a belfry rising through the roof in the manner of a church steeple.

Revenue paid a passing glance to it and no more, for the lane had abruptly thrust him into a compound-like yard filled with loitering men. Obeying the strict etiquette of the range, he wheeled the horse to put his gun side away from them and waited for an invitation to dismount.

The invitation was a long time coming, though he soon enough realized it was not from oversight. Fifteen-odd punchers shifted position to affix a studied, unsmiling scrutiny on him. The interval of silence dragged out. Revenue stiffened his slim six feet and mentally observed: "Hard lot —and bad manners." But the lean, bronzed gravity of his cheeks remained unchanged.

Sitting there, he was a character not to be mistaken. Texas had produced and nurtured him. Its hot sun had lifted him toward the sky, pinched in his girth and flattened his muscles. It had sharpened his features and given to him an air of laconic certainty. All about him was the emanation of a serene capability tempered by reserve, as if long ago he had learned that personal safety was forever a matter of doubt.

Nobody in the crowd moved or spoke, but a man came swiftly around the corner of the main house and advanced on Revenue. A few yards off he halted and studied the newcomer with an extraordinary sharpness. His was a slight, whiplike figure with the obvious bearing of impatient and arbitrary authority. After a time, in which he seemed to satisfy some inner doubt, the lines of his taciturn face settled and he spoke.

"Light and rest."

Revenue made another mental reservation. "He's from Texas, not long enough ago to get his drawl filed off." Aloud he said: "Thanks kindly. My horse—"

The man turned to the crowd, snapping out an order. "Joe, take this pony."

Revenue stepped to earth and stamped the stiffness out of his legs.

The other man's glance ran intently up and down the Texan and his eyes, cold green, settled on the Texan's features. "You had a hot day for riding, brother."

"Not one, but many," mused Revenue.

"I judged that."

Revenue grinned, upon which fine wrinkles broke about the corners of his eyes. "Can't conceal the mark of the south, I'll admit. I'm a long ways from Texas."

"Texas," muttered the man, and his face grew together, darker and more bitter. "What part?"

"Different parts," was Revenue's laconic answer. "You're from thataway yourself."

The man's reply was swift and curt. "Not for a good many years, friend. And don't mention the damned state to me."

"It affects some like that," agreed Revenue, the grin fading. "What outfit's this?"

"Rafter T—Colonel Fulk Trevison, owner. I'm foreman. Al LeGrue is the name."

"I'd admire to ride for you," said Revenue. "Got to get a job some place and it might as well be here. Call me Mark Revenue and you'll be approximately correct."

LeGrue stood still, but his lids drew up, and Revenue had a full view of the peculiarly arctic green of the eyes. No kind warmth or compassion existed in them, nor any humor or friendliness. Moreover, as he watched, Revenue saw the chill expression spreading outward and fixing lip, nostril and cheek muscles in a frozen attitude. LeGrue seemed to be waiting for further talk, seemed to expect it. Both arms hung by his gunbelt, as stiff as the rest of his body. Utter silence fell over the yard, broken only by the chatter of water falling into a trough. All this occupied but a moment, yet Revenue felt the strain distinctly and it set him on guard; so much so that when the ranch bell clanged again the sound of it dragged across his nerves.

LeGrue suddenly dropped his eyes and muttered a short oath. "Come and eat. We'll talk about that job later."

Revenue followed the foreman across the yard and into a long wing off the house, nor did he fail to note that the crew hung back until LeGrue had entered. Once more he laid away a shrewd observation. "Hard bunch, but LeGrue's harder. What in hell am I in?"

The foreman took his place at the head of the table and motioned Revenue to the nearest right-hand seat with a brief remark. "Owner never eats with us. Powerful set man, Trevison. Pitch in."

It was a silent meal and soon done. None of the easygoing and jovial comment of the average ranch group passed around this table. Men ate with their heads down, silently, like dogs wolfing out of a common pan and surlily afraid of missing their share. At odd occasions a brief grunt broke from one or another throat and the echo of it struck barrenly along the walls, actually seeming to be smothered and repelled by the heavy, sullen air hanging over the place. Then, as impatiently as they had sat down, these uncommunicative men rose to file out.

Revenue, setting his pace by that of the foreman, was glad likewise to leave so cheerless a dining room behind. Bright day had departed, the rearing mountain wall was a shifting mass of purple shadow. In the valley one long surviving streamer of light gradually faded to evening haze. An alpine chill streamed down from the peaks, cutting through Revenue's flat frame and touching his thin southern blood.

LeGrue lit a cigarette and swung about to face the Texan. "A job, huh?"

"Yeah," said Revenue.

LeGrue raised his voice. "Joe, get this man's saddle and put it on Pliny!" Then motioning Revenue to follow, he walked toward the open mouth of a shed, still with the air of hurried impatience. Men followed casually. LeGrue went inside the barn and reappeared with a coiled, limp buckskin rope. This he handed to Revenue and pointed along the yard. Thirty feet away a bale of hay rested with its broadest side to the earth, and projecting diagonally from the two near corners was a pair of sticks—a dummy cow with dummy horns.

It was a common practice target all along the Western range and Revenue, smiling slightly, shook out his loop and built it up to a diagonal spin. It amused him to consider that Rafter T put its prospective hands through the paces before hiring them and, as a gesture of self-confidence, he retreated another five feet and whipped the loop higher in preparation for the launching.

At that moment one of the crew walked up to the bale and swiftly pushed it over, thus changing the plane of the target and leaving but one horn to shoot at. Revenue was on the verge of letting go when the change occurred; he shifted his body slightly, overset the loop with a snap of his wrist and threw. The loop fell neatly and accurately on the prong.

"Was that part of the test," he drawled, "or is our friend being funny?"

The man by the bale, who was thin and pale-cheeked, shot a dark glance at Revenue. "Make any difference to you, mister, which it was?"

"Might," was Revenue's laconic answer.

LeGrue snapped at the puncher. "Get out of the way, Badger. Revenue, when we take a hand on Rafter T he's got to expect anything. Come along."

They went around the barn and walked through the flaring wings of a corral. LeGrue opened the gate and stepped aside, saying, "There it is, brother, and you don't have to ride it if you're careful minded." Then he closed the gate and Revenue stood inside.

The top bar of the corral was lined with the Rafter T crew looking silently on. Dust rolled from the center of the arena, kicked up by the fiddling feet of a gray and gaunt brute of a horse whose ears were flat and whose nostrils flared. He was saddled and held to the snubbing post by a round turn of a hackamore rope. Behind the post, crouching watchfully and holding the free end of the rope, was the puncher Joe who earlier had taken Revenue's pony away.

Revenue's lips tightened and he ran another glance around the roosting circle of men. All along that ring of dark, unsmiling faces he observed a common expression of expectancy and brutal desire. Nowhere was a flash of friendly feeling. He unhooked his gunbelt, laid it over the gate, and rubbed his hands dry. "The innocent stranger," said he, to himself, "makes a Roman holiday." Then, across the corral, he thought he detected one lone man faintly shaking his head as a kind of undercover warning. One lone man with yellow hair gleaming in the dusk. But if it were a warning meant in honest spirit, it soon enough disappeared, leaving only a mask of gravity. Revenue drew a breath and walked nearer the horse.

There was a lunge and a flash of hind feet. Revenue stepped away, catlike, and waited. The horse circled the snubbing post and stopped. Revenue came in again and put out his arm tentatively. The brute seemed to settle, all muscles growing taut.

The man holding the snubbing hackamore rope muttered, "That's his custom, he won't move now till you're on his back."

"And then the stars fall down," murmured Revenue, placing one foot in the near stirrup. He exerted a slight pressure, tarried a brief instant and vaulted to the saddle. Settling his other foot, he bent over and took a grip on the tight hackamore rope. "Let go," said he. The puncher obeyed and scrambled for the corral wall. Revenue straightened and let his spurs fall. The horse trembled, shot clear of the post, reared high up and came down convulsively. Revenue's neck snapped, his head rang. The evening dusk seemed to swirl more heavily around the corral and for one flickering interval of time he saw men's set cheeks turned on him and lips curled back.

Then the horse shot toward the corral's side and threw one flank against it, essaying to crush or scrape Revenue; the latter lifted his leg. He felt the animal's mighty muscles surge and he tried to ram his boot back in the dangling stirrup. The horse rocketed across the dust, plunging from one violent arc to another, shaking himself at each mad heave. Men on the corral rim capsized from sight as the horse, lusting to destroy, struck the barrier once more.

13

Revenue, both feet now out of stirrups, chose that moment to depart; he hit the dirt flatly, rolled sidewise and got up on the run, aiming for the corral gate and his holstered gun hanging there. A single shout of warning broke behind him as he reached his objective and snatched the gun free. There was a pounding and a roaring, and when he turned, the black shadow of the horse rose enormously and terrifically against the darkening sky; Revenue backed off, firing directly into the enraged animal's chest. The horse came down, legs giving way, body rolling and a sound half a scream and half a roar guttering out of its throat. Dust rolled thickly and silence settled like a blanket.

Revenue checked his hard breathing. "Was that something else I was supposed to expect?" he challenged. "If so, you'll observe how I rise to reply. There'll be no more suckers risking their necks on that half ton of iniquity. LeGrue, if it's your bright idea I don't think much of it."

The corral gate swung open. LeGrue stood before him. The shadows were deepening all around and the foreman's face seemed to absorb part of the darkness. All Revenue saw clearly was a mouth pressed tight and wide green eyes flickering.

"I knew he was bad," said LeGrue, "but I didn't put him in the man-killer class. No hard feelings for killing him. I'd done it myself. You're hired. Come to the big house with me."

Revenue's slow temper had risen and it was on his tongue to say he wanted no job on the Rafter T. But some impulse stayed the words and he fell in step beside LeGrue, going back around the barn and across the yard to the porch of the ranch house.

LeGrue spoke softly. "The old man's a hard number. Pay no heed to any undue remarks. Just forget 'em if he makes any. He's a man-killer himself."

A voice emerged from the porch—a slow, half whining voice. "What was that shooting, LeGrue?"

LeGrue spoke with soft deference. "Pliny tried to massacre this man, Colonel. Had to shoot him. Here's a new hand for the outfit. He'll do, Colonel."

There was a shaft of lamplight cutting out of the open door, and because of its glaring brilliance against the descending background of night Revenue's eyes were blurred. All he saw of this Colonel Fulk Trevison was a rounded bulk sitting in a chair and an enormous head supporting a shock of hair that seemed to be white. The owner's voice came again, thin and reedy.

"Is he good, LeGrue? You know him? Is he right? You know what I mean—is he right?"

"He'll do, Colonel," repeated LeGrue, bearing down on the words.

The owner stirred. "Young man, I can't see you. Eyes poor. But if LeGrue says you're right, that's good with me. I want you to remember that this is a hard outfit to work for and there is one strict rule no man dares break. Keep your mouth shut. Believe nothing you hear about Rafter T, repeat nothing you hear around Rafter T."

Silence fell. Revenue, weighing every word spoken by the two men, was aware of some unsaid thought dominating them. The oppressive air seemed to hang thicker over the yard, influencing owner and foreman as well as crew. Some sinister shadow, some mark of blood, some ghostly presence clung to the ranch like an actual being.

LeGrue nudged Revenue and they walked away. "He's mild tonight," muttered LeGrue. "A hard man is Trevison."

There was a rising of hoof echoes. Revenue stepped aside to let a quartet of horsemen slide abreast and halt. He saw these four figures all cloaked against the increasing cold, gunbelts strapped outside the extra clothing, and a rifle slung from each pommel.

LeGrue was murmuring: "Clear along the bench tonight, all the way from No-Speak Pass to Peepsight. Don't stop to stamp your feet. Keep moving." Then the party slipped away and LeGrue had lifted his voice to reach around the yard. "Tomorrow's the beginning of roundup, so we'll hit town tonight for a bender. Them as wants to go, saddle up!"

"I'll trail along," mused Revenue.

"I judged," said LeGrue. "There's a fresh horse by the gate with your saddle already on it." He walked into the darkness beside the corral; a sound of swearing rose from it and of ponies pitching. Lights burned more brightly in the bunkhouse, men hurried past Revenue, leaving him alone and gripped by hard, swift thoughts. A cold wave of warning poured over him.

"I want none of this," he thought. "Not any. None." There was a taint to the job given him, a hidden string attached to it. Better get to his own horse and split away before he had penetrated too far into the affairs of Rafter T and so had become a partner to whatever queer, sinister things these brooding men were mixed in. Better to withdraw in grace than by later gunplay, such as his own knowledge of the range told him would immediately develop. On impulse he wheeled and started after LeGrue.

He took only a step when a clear, slow feminine voice floated over the yard, stopping him in his tracks, turning him around to face the porch. The words were distinct: "Dad, will there never be an end to this!" And there were other phrases, too, running hurriedly together in one gust of breath. There was a girl standing in the light of the doorway, body silhouetted. Both of her arms were lifted to her breast, and as he watched, startled out of his own forebodings, he saw her head drop forward. A stifled, despairing cry lifted through the silence and died abruptly.

LeGrue was returning, leading a pair of horses. "Hop on," said the foreman, "and let's depart."

Revenue mounted and fell into the tail of the procession. It filed through the gate and veered north with men ranking two by two and a wild, ribald yell beating high. The pace increased. To the left reared the black mountain wall, peak tops making dim spires against a sky aglitter with stars; to the right and to the front was open valley. The man abreast of him lit a match to a cigarette and by the flittering, momentary glow Revenue recognized the face of that yellow-haired individual who had seemed to try to nod a warning at him in the corral.

Soft words reached across. "You're lucky—and again you ain't. Know anything about this country, Revenue?"

CHAPTER 2

Revenue put a little pressure into one knee and threw his horse nearer this yellow-haired man. The sweep of the wind and the murmur of the cavalcade's free-running travel damped his words. "Where was the luck?"

"In passing through the Rafter T gate without being shot. In getting that Pliny brute before he got you. He's a killer."

"Nice outfit," observed Revenue. "And how am I unlucky?"

The answer was delayed. Turning his head, Revenue saw the young man staring into the crystal starlight. Presently the latter said, "Try and quit this ranch. You'll see then."

"Don't recall signing any enlistment papers."

"Just try to draw out," insisted the man. After a further silence he added, "My name's Nick Salt. I come up from the Nations country six months ago. I was lucky getting through that front gate, too."

16

Revenue made a chance shot. "And had no luck trying to depart?"

"I know better than to declare my intentions," said Salt very swiftly. "Men before me have tried it. Seeing as what happened to them, I just trail along and keep my mouth shut."

"Nice outfit," repeated Revenue. "A nice little flytrap."

"Mantrap," said Salt definitely and broke off speaking. They had fallen a little behind the column. A rider in the lead drew out and slowed, coming abreast of them. It was LeGrue and he set his pace beside Revenue, saying nothing at all. But the effect of his presence was to leave Revenue with a sense of being oppressed and threatened; and as the latter rode along, his temper began to stir again, chafing at the restraint. The girl and her sudden, agitated phrases disturbed him tremendously. Tragedy hovered over the Rafter T—tragedy and mystery.

A long, wild yell rose from the head of the column. In the middle distance winked town lights, like stars floating down from the sky. LeGrue pulled ahead, the column swung to another direction as if aiming to circle around, and the pace increased.

"Firehole town yonder," muttered Nick Salt. Then, with a sudden burst of bitterness, he ground out an oath. "Damn his heart! Damn his butchering soul!"

The party swept toward Firehole, spurring hard. The yelling rose stronger and a gun cracked into the sky. Revenue, who had been on hell-bent expeditions of this nature before, pulled his horse out of the column a little way and ran abreast. His experience had been that these long suffering cowtowns occasionally rose up in wrath and shot an outfit to pieces. From his vantage point he saw an outline of buildings ahead of him, split in the center by a wide street; and he saw men running rapidly down it, bound for shelter. Lights died one after another, a wagon and team raced away, going around a corner madly. Thus Firehole prepared for its company, seeming to crouch and huddle in fear. The cavalcade entered the street end with every Rafter T man swaying in the saddle and every gun blasting the echoes. Revenue checked and walked his pony toward a dark hotel porch, leaving the crew to its own pleasures. Dismounting, he found a chair and sat down.

"They been held in so tight they're half crazy," he reflected.

The cavalcade ran the length of the street, turned and charged back. Bullets were no longer being directed straight up, but into the building sides. Revenue heard the smash of wood, the cries of men who seemed bent more on destruction than pleasure. Muzzle lights puffed out, pale blue and crimson. Still in compact formation, the bunch galloped past him, wheeled and went one by one into the saloon opposite. The swinging doors began to splinter and then were unhinged, turning to kindling wood under trampling hoofs. He could see them inside, riding around and around the room, upsetting tables and chairs. Glass shattered; a pair of riders came out, ropes dragging some heavy object and in a moment the saloon's piano, bereft of one leg, capsized in the dust. More shots exploded riotously.

LeGrue apparently had not led the way into the saloon, for he now emerged from an alley between buildings, dismounted and stopped by the wrecked swinging doors. A moment later he wheeled away as if struck by a sudden thought and looked around the street. His attention fell on Revenue's horse. Directly afterward he walked to the hotel porch. Revenue saw the man's face to be intently set, brooding, and very watchful.

"Not joining the party, Revenue?"

"In due time," drawled the latter.

"Better get your fill now," warned LeGrue. "It's a long dry spell on the ranch."

"If I go back," said Revenue.

LeGrue stiffened. "You'll go back. You got a job."

"Not quite sure. Haven't made up my mind yet."

"You'll go back," repeated LeGrue. "I said you would."

He waited for an answer. None came. Revenue's cigarette tip glowed brightly and his long body rested quiescent in the chair. The Rafter T foreman swung on his heel and marched over to the saloon, entering. A sound of brawling and cursing emerged, of men deep in drink and already growing surly. Something happened yonder. There was a rush for the door; one man backed out, slugging the air with his fists. Then LeGrue appeared, leaping at the other. He struck like a cat, each blow echoing along the street. He circled, leaped again, hit his man across the back of the neck with his forearm. The man wilted in the dust.

"Do what I tell you to do!" breathed LeGrue. "Get up or I'll grind your belly with my heel!"

The man rose, shook himself together and entered the saloon. A few moments later he came out with a partner, both of them in the saddle. They split, one going to each end of the street. Revenue saw them halt and take up guard. Very quietly he ground his cigarette on the porch rail.

"So he intends for me to go back—and no place else."

Revenue started to rise, the slow temper in him boiling dangerously. But in another instant the street was flooded with Rafter T men. They careened through the saloon doorway on foot, jostling each other, crying out a common thought: "Get that marshal!"

Past the saloon they ran. Three buildings onward they came to a turbulent pause.

"Door's locked!"

"Knock it down, then!"

"Ryan, you putty-spined, stinking, spit-licking star-toter—open that door afore we bust it down!"

A resolute, calming voice answered them from inside the building which Revenue judged to be the jail. "Ease off, boys. You're not going to set any of my star boarders free this trip. Go drink it off."

"Bust it down and drag him out!"

The locked door rattled to a strenuous battering, but held fast. Apparently the forewarned marshal had set up a barricade, which was undoubtedly an error of judgment. To the milling men it was raw meat, a challenge to their wildness. One of the party ran back, got his horse and returned on the gallop. He stood up in his saddle, reached the iron grating of an upper window and passed his rope through. The idea caught on and was vigorously applauded. Another rider swung beside him and another rope was anchored to the grating. Then both men settled in their saddles and took up the slack.

"Ready—heave!"

The grating gave and fell with a crash. Instantly the crowd pushed a man upward. He broke the glass with his gunbutt, knocked in the supporting ribs of the window and crawled through the aperture. Others followed him. An explosion of shots shook the jail's interior, boots raced down a stairway. The doorway came open, to admit a thoroughly aroused Rafter T outfit. Immediately thereafter furniture flew out, to be dashed against the ground and broken by a waiting puncher. More glass showered down from other second-story openings and mattresses were hurled to the street. A thick and passionate shouting rose thunderously.

"Ryan—where's Ryan? Get him!"

But the marshal apparently had taken his leave, for no sound of discovery emerged. However, the jail was being competently and enthusiastically wrecked. Nothing, it appeared to the listening Revenue, remained unbroken that the wild ones could get their hands on; and it even seemed they were ripping away the inner walls of the place.

Al LeGrue came from the saloon, wiping his mouth with

the back of a coat sleeve. He entered the jail, and emerged a little later on the run. "Salt—where are you?"

There was no answer. LeGrue yelled angrily, "Salt!" Then he dived into the jail again, bellowing. Men began to stream out of it, sprawling over one another. LeGrue made his exit furiously. "Get me a lantern!" he bawled. "Salt, where you gone?"

A man raced for the saloon, returning with a lantern. One of the guards galloped in from the street end. "Somebody went to the stable," said he. LeGrue broke into a lumbering trot with the outfit at his back and aimed for the black maw of a stable door farther away from the jail. The lantern swayed, was carried through the door and shut from Revenue's observation. The Rafter T men halted restlessly. LeGrue's hard, threatening words floated back. "So—trying to get another horse and sneak out on me, uh, Salt?"

Salt's reply was touched with desperation. "By God, I'm through! This is a free country."

"Sure. Nothing to stop you from quitting if that's your desire. But you'll do your quitting at the ranch. When I take an outfit to town I bring it back—*in toto*. Forget it. We're riding home."

Revenue rose from his chair with sudden quietness and went down the street. Men made a dense wall across the stable door. Over their heads he saw Nick Salt standing at bay, the pleasant face drawn and a little pale, but pressed together in determination. One hand held the reins of a saddled and waiting horse. But for premature discovery he probably would have gone through the back of the stable and made his escape. LeGrue confronted him, hands akimbo. Another man stood near, holding up the lantern.

"To hell with you," said Salt. "I'm through. You won't get me back to the ranch."

"You'll come back," insisted LeGrue. "I always bring the same number home that I leave with. There's your war bag and your pay, too. Wouldn't leave them behind, would you?"

"Keep the money," muttered Salt. "It's worth that much to me to get the stink of the place outa my nose. I don't fall into the trap again, LeGrue."

"What would Colonel Trevison say to me if I didn't see you got home?" was LeGrue's ironic question.

"Trevison," snorted Salt. "Hell, ain't that a funny number? No, I'm leaving right now."

"Not in a thousand years. You're coming with me. Make up your mind."

Revenue pushed his way through the crowd, went past LeGrue and turned to face the foreman, thus placing himself beside Salt. That puncher shot an inquiring glance at Revenue.

LeGrue scowled and grunted, "Well, what you want?"

"Thought he might like a little moral support," drawled Revenue. "Neither one of us is going back, LeGrue."

Salt let out a long breath of air. LeGrue's grim lips became one thin and bloodless line across his scowling face. A flash and flare of killer spirit turned his cold green eyes to so much glass. Standing immovable he droned out his words.

"You boys have had your fun. That's all you're going to have. I brought you to town. I'm taking you back. Do your quitting to Trevison, not to me."

"Go back to be slaughtered!" cried Nick Salt. "Like others! Not me!"

"Last warning," stated LeGrue. "Step out of this stable right now or take the consequences. Nobody monkeys with me." And as he said it he seemed to set, to compress his muscles. There was a dragging silence, a silence in which men labored for breath and in which the moments seemed to sag with the heavy freight of disaster.

Never daring to remove his attention from LeGrue, Revenue sized up his chances rapidly. Salt was rooted to the spot, an arm's length away. To Salt's left, and to be reached in one good jump, was the partial protection of an empty stall. To his own right a tall pile of baled hay created an angle where he might find shelter, if he could but reach it. The Rafter T man holding the lantern inched nearer him and a little bit farther from LeGrue; back of the foreman was a mass of staring faces emitting a common air of wolfish desire.

"Would you go to the gun?" asked Revenue.

LeGrue's voice was rough with strain. "I'll take you back or see you dead."

The man holding the lantern edged still farther from LeGrue, coming directly opposite Revenue. Revenue passed a hand across his forehead as if to clear his eyes of light blur; the hand ran slowly from temple to temple, sprang to flashing speed, slashed over the interval and ripped the lantern bail from the holder's loose grasp. Salt yelled and moved. The lantern went smashing against LeGrue's shoulder, globe breaking and light turning a weird purple in the air. LeGrue whirled to clear himself as darkness fell; and Revenue, reaching the protection of the baled hay, heard the Rafter T outfit cursing its way wildly out of the stable. A gunshot crashed through the place.

Revenue held his fire, calling out. "All right, Salt?"

The puncher's reply was dry and confident: "Yeah."

LeGrue had retreated, the rest of the Rafter T men were in the street and clear of the door. LeGrue yelled savagely, "I'll burn this damned thing down just to see you singe!"

"Two men are as good as two dozen at this business," retorted Revenue. "Make up your mind—we're not joining Rafter T. Better bust the dust before a few more folks in town decide to join our party."

LeGrue said nothing. He seemed to be collecting his outfit at a farther removed vantage point.

Salt whispered, "Here I come," and ran across to the pile of bales. "We better mooch out of this before they surround us."

"Bright idea," agreed Revenue.

Together, they ran through the stable and passed the rear door. Beyond were the ragged skeletons of a series of corrals. Salt seemed to know where he wanted to go and Revenue accordingly followed him down the building ends, turned into an alleyway and pressed forward. They stood, presently, at the margin of town, commanding a fair view. The Rafter T was asaddle and waiting.

LeGrue's high, vindictive challenge came clearly to them: "You're marked from this minute on! I'll see you both run to earth!"

"God bless you for the sweet sentiments," murmured Revenue.

The Rafter T turned and ran impetuously away from Firehole. The trembling reverberation of pony hoofs diminished and died. Silence settled, a kind of fluttering calm returned to the town.

Revenue and Salt sat on their heels in the dark and waited while lights sprang up from building to building and citizens began venturing from shelter. Somebody passed them, cursing with a wholehearted vigor.

"A bowl of beans wouldn't go bad," reflected Revenue.

"Hollow as a drum," corroborated Salt. "Why in hell did you risk your neck in my business?"

"Seemed logical. Both of us had the same business, didn't we—which was to sunder the binding ties with Mister LeGrue."

"No mistake," gloomed Salt, "I was in a hole and no ladder to climb out. He had me on his hip."

"And still you aimed to scrap it out," admired Revenue.

"Well, I had declared myself. Couldn't back down. What I wanted right then was a pair of wings." He paused, then added gruffly, "I'm obliged to you, Revenue. I'm in debt to you."

Revenue passed it off laconically. "We'll discharge the

obligation over the beans. Question now arises, how safe is this man's town?"

"Rafter T has got no friends here, if that's what you want to know."

"After this evening's performance I don't see how it could have," opined Revenue.

"But that won't prevent LeGrue from trying to sneak back and surprise us. He's a fellow pretty set in his ways."

Silence piled up again. A quarter hour passed. Revenue rolled a cigarette, smoked it, ground it into the dust. "Let's surround them beans. My hunch is he won't come back to-night. Anyhow, I'd rather be shot than go hungry."

They advanced along the street, keeping well to the thicker shadows of the sidewalk. Townsmen roamed from building to building and their talk clashed and snapped with anger. Coming abreast of the open door of a restaurant, the two turned in and sat down. There was a wall lamp directly above the table which Revenue carefully attended, screwing the wick down until the flame was but a raveling wisp. A gaunt and solemn man in a dirty apron approached suspiciously.

"Back door lead through the kitchen?" queried Revenue.

"A-huh," admitted the proprietor.

"Good. If you see a couple of fast shadows go through it, that's us. Here's a dollar in advance. Bring on the beans."

The proprietor retreated. Salt, facing the door, laid his gun on the table and grinned cheerfully. "Revenue, you're a cool cucumber. It's a God's mercy we ain't both fit subjects for a funeral sermon."

Revenue liked the man increasingly. He wore well. He had a good, lean jaw, a clear, candid glance and the hint of crowtracks at the corner of each eye. There was a set to him, a robust confidence and the unmistakable air of honesty. Revenue dug into a bowl of oyster cracks and laconically wrote off the recent episode. "Well, we got through it and we still live."

"We're not through with this yet," warned Salt. "I know LeGrue. He'll do what he says he'll do. He'll move through hell and high water to get us. This country ain't a safe place for you nor me from now on."

"Too bad. I'm planning to stick around a while."

"All right. Double the statement for me then."

It was Salt's declaration of partnership. Revenue accepted it gravely. "Good enough. What I want to know is, why is this LeGrue specimen so all-fired reluctant to lose his punchers? I never had to use a can opener before to get out of a job."

Salt held his tongue while the restaurant man dumped

23

plates of provender on the table and departed with the attitude of one having quitted a disagreeable chore. "Same question," said Salt in a low tone, "as I have asked m'self ever since I started working for that outfit. I'm some wiser now, but don't know anything more than in the beginning."

"This Trevison must be a woolly wampus from Bitter Creek," suggested Revenue.

"Yeah? He's a round fat man with a squeaky voice and walks like he was trying to lose his shadder."

"Not according to LeGrue's estimate."

"I know," muttered Salt. "LeGrue plays him as a man-eater. There's something else funny. And while we're on the subject, LeGrue picks the men and does the hiring. Trevison only nods. They don't hire from this country, either. It's always a sucker like you or me, fresh off the trail and strange to the country."

"And nobody quits?"

"Nope. They have accidents and die. Usually out in the hills."

Revenue considered this thoughtfully and long. Salt shook his head. "You'd think a man would catch on after five or six months at a place. But I didn't. Nobody talks around there. The fear of God is just naturally planted in 'em by this LeGrue. Mostly, they're old hands. I heard once LeGrue joined Trevison a long time back with several partners. I dunno. All I can swear to is he picks his men awful careful and keeps 'em."

"There would be one answer," suggested Revenue.

"Rustling? Nope. Not in my time. I'd be a dumb one if I didn't make that. They got lots of beef up in the meadows beyond No-Speak Pass. But it's legitimate. And there's another item. They guard that country like it was paved with diamonds. Just try and get in there sometime."

"Other ranches near by?"

"Few and far between. This is new country. Trevison was a first settler. Firehole town is only about five years old. They were potting Indians up until real recent."

They were on the point of rising to leave when a ruddy man with wrestler's shoulders came in. "Listen," he ordered, "if you got any trouble with LeGrue, get out of town sudden. I won't stand for another brawl around here."

"All right, Ryan," agreed Salt, "we wouldn't sleep here anyhow."

"Ought to run you in on general principles," growled the marshal. "Just for belonging to such a poisonous outfit. One of these days I aim to collect a party and blast that bunch to hell and gone."

Salt's answer was accompanied by a gentle grin. "You mean you can *try*." The partners rose and left the restaurant. Quite unconsciously leadership fell on the tall Texan, for Salt looked up to him and asked: "Well, what now?"

"We're afoot, which is bad," reflected Revenue. "And we're in a poor place to camp. Better to sleep out on the prairie. Item one is horseflesh."

"You wait here," said Salt and walked toward the stable. Revenue rolled a cigarette and stared down the street. A moment later the marshal came from the restaurant.

"Been in these parts long?" questioned Revenue.

"Matters of years," admitted Ryan, neither friendly nor unfriendly. He looked sharply at Revenue.

"Most of the Montana-bound trail herds pass through here, don't they?"

"Yeah."

"Ever see one known as the Arrow outfit?"

The marshal reflected. "When would that a-been?"

"Three years ago."

"Never come through here," stated the marshal. "What was the owner's name?"

"Revenue."

"Nope," said the marshal and, seeing something down the street that interested him, he walked away. Revenue shook his head.

"Funny. Damned funny. Trail just peters out in these parts." Then Revenue moved into a store adjacent to the restaurant. When he emerged five minutes later he had a gunnysack partially filled with provisions. Salt was back, holding a pair of ponies.

"Pays to have friends," said he.

The two mounted and swung from the town's northern edge. Salt, knowing the country, accepted the lead and aimed toward the black mass of mountains on the west. About three miles out he drew up before a stream that ran between moderately high banks. "Good enough?" he inquired.

"Slick," agreed Revenue, dismounting. He stood there a long while, listening to the stray sounds coming through the night. Salt rode down a small trail and threw a fire together that was concealed from the rest of the world. Presently Revenue joined him, unsaddled and put his pony on a picket. He dropped to his heels before the blaze, soberly watching Salt across the flame points. The scrutiny was so sober and direct that Salt grew restless.

"Now what've I done?" he wanted to know.

"Got yourself in a bad jam," drawled Revenue.

Salt's brows arched. Reserve came to his face. "As how?"

CHAPTER 3

Revenue stared into the fire. He had laced his strong, long-fingered hands together. The light of the flames hollowed out his cheeks and accented the bold modeling of nose and chin and mouth. By dark his air of careless ease was lost and the level gray eyes were infinitely harder of expression.

"Anybody," he presently remarked, "is in for a lot of grief when they ride with me. I'm looking for a particular brand of trouble."

Salt let out a breath. "Hell, you had me worried. Thought you was a highbinder for a minute. Since I bought a stack in this game, what's the deal?"

Revenue descended into a deep study, appearing not to hear Salt's question. But after a long silence he pulled himself upright, as if having made a decision.

"All right," he said. "You're in on this, so here goes. I'm looking for an outfit of fourteen men and five thousand head of beef which left Texas three years ago for Montana range and never was heard about since."

"Good gravy," murmured Salt. "Whose outfit?"

"My father's," said Revenue, features sharpening. "We had a fine range down south. Dad ran it well, with a couple of my younger brothers. But north is the place to put weight on beef and so he got the idea of changing location. He had a place in Montana picked out. Then he sold our old range, gathered up everything and set out up the trail. Three years ago. Not a word, not a line, not a hint since as to what happened to him. All I know is he never got to Montana."

"Where was you all this time?" asked Salt.

"That's the hell of it," muttered Revenue. "I was the drifter in our family. Always wanted to see what grew on the other side of the hill. Dad figured me to take over the outfit. Hurt him when I kept foraying from pillar to post. That's what influenced him to move. I was away at the time he pulled out. Hadn't been home for almost a year. And when I did pull into the old front yard, two more years had gone by—which was about the length of time he'd been gone. It was somebody else's front yard then. Nothing left for me but a letter telling where I'd find him in Montana."

"So you went to Montana?"

"Yeah. But he never had got there. Me, I set out to travel the trail back. That's a year ago. I been on every fork of the

Chisholm since then. No trace. Not until I drifted up this way. He'd been through Dodge, all right. And lost a couple of his old hands there in a shooting scrape. He'd hit Ogallala, followed the north bank of the Platte and hit Cheyenne. I pieced it out. Then everything just petered out. Fifty miles below here I found an old freighter who remembered seeing the herd. After that, nothing. Something happened to fourteen men and five thousand cattle. Wiped out, swallowed up, disappeared. Not a hide nor hair nor smell."

"Figure that!" grunted Salt.

"There's just three things I can figure. No, four. First, a stampede scattered the outfit from hell to breakfast. But that's a slim chance. He was an old hand and wouldn't lose everything thataway. Second, cholera might've struck the outfit. There was some of it on the trail then. But it seems there'd be a story left somewhere if such a thing happened. Third, he might've met a fellow in the feeder business, got a good price and sold out. Naturally the men would scatter, but it seems likely some of 'em would hit back to Texas. No, that ain't a good answer, either."

Silence dropped again.

Salt said, "Well, what's left?"

"One more way to look at it," replied Revenue. "That he was sliced to pieces by trail rustlers somewhere within fifty miles or a hundred miles of this spot. I believe it. I'm looking for evidence of it. There must be something or somebody left. And I tell you, Salt, if I ever find a clue I'll hunt it down until the ground runs red!"

"So that's what I bought for my money?"

"Declare yourself out if you want, old man."

Salt reared up. "Hell, don't talk thataway. I'm in with both feet. What comes next?"

Revenue moved his arm in the direction of the rearing shadows. "Up yonder is a rugged country. I want to look through it. I want to poke into the high valleys. Five thousand head of stock couldn't sink into the earth. There's bound to be a trace of 'em somewhere. And around here some place is the end of the trail. I'm sure about that."

"You'd know that old crew, wouldn't you?"

"Part of it, but not all. Remember, I wasn't home for a year. The outfit could have changed a lot in that time. But there's some old-timers I know wouldn't have quit."

Salt held his peace for a while, then said: "Reason I asked was on account of LeGrue. If he'd been with your dad's outfit—"

"The idea has occurred to me," admitted Revenue. "But I never saw him before."

"It keeps sticking in my mind," persisted Salt. "There's something all-fired queer about the Rafter T. I never could get a word from anybody. LeGrue's a man-killer and he sure put the fear of God in the bunch. Nobody talked. It ain't natural."

"That's the reason I want to get up into those peaks," said Revenue.

"We'll have a sweet time," gloomed Salt. "LeGrue guards the passes close. There's a line cabin and a man at each entrance to Rafter T range. They ain't letting anybody in. Even in case we get through secretly, it's an even break we're spotted. You know what they do then? Lay down a rifle fire thick enough to kill flies. I seen it done once. I was on patrol, too. I had to flop on my belly and shoot at a poor devil. They got him cold. Only satisfaction is knowing it wasn't my slug which killed him. I aimed wide. But there's warning for you."

"What's LeGrue's alibi for pulling that kind of a stunt?" asked Revenue.

"Afraid of rustlers, he says. Mebbe, I dunno. It's a tough, wild country."

"We'll tackle it," said Revenue.

"Right with you," agreed Salt.

Talk died and the fire settled to a round, crimson disk of ashes. The partners rolled up in their blankets for the night. Out from the high range came a stiff, cold wind that ruffled the creek's surface. Mark Revenue, smoking the last of his cigarette, listened for a while to the stray sounds running past, then fell asleep.

Revenue was lifted bodily from slumber by the sound of horses splashing across the creek not a hundred feet away. The warning brought him bolt upright in his blankets, staring along the gloom-ridden trough of the stream; and from his vantage point he saw them dimly stretched out in a line as they came down the incline and stopped at the water— four riders sitting slack in their saddles. Their mounts were drinking and in the pause he made out the drowsy drawl of their fragmentary talk.

". . . Swing along the base and hit home."

"Ride all night, work all day."

"Choke it off. Bad talk for you, boy."

"Ain't it right? You know it's right."

"Go ahead, you fool, and get advertised to LeGrue. Get advertised to him—and get killed."

"You bet, kid. Hush your mouth."

Revenue's attention snapped to the fire, thinking that it must surely betray him. But, like all suddenly awakened sleepers, he had misjudged elapsed time. Instead of a few moments, a matter of hours had passed and the embers of the blaze were stone cold, long dead.

Salt's torso reared near at hand; a muted whisper came to Revenue. "Rafter T patrol."

Revenue's hand reached out beside him and lifted his gun. A spasm of cold shook him and his thin southern blood seemed congealed. The patrol party started on across the creek, and then it was that one of the partners' ponies, catching the scent of his own species, broke the covert quiet with a soft whicker. Revenue flung his blanket aside and placed himself flat against the overhanging bank.

The members of the patrol wheeled, facing in. A blunt challenge shot forward. "Who's that? Sing out!"

Revenue drawled, "Can't a man bed down for the night without being disturbed? On your way and don't make so damned much noise."

"What you doing here? What's your name?"

"Same questions, right back at you," said Revenue. "Go on, mind your business and I'll do likewise. It's a good time to let well enough alone."

"We'll have to take a look," said another voice. "Come on over here."

"You're dragging too much rope," retorted Revenue. "Go home and sleep it off."

There was a momentary pause. Out of it fell a brittle phrase. "Swallow this pill then." And the cold brooding calm of the night was shattered by the flat echo of a gun. Revenue saw the mushrooming muzzle light flicker and vanish. Before he could reply Salt had moved into action with a wicked, headlong fire. The patrol members surged up the bank, answering in kind; and as the last rider topped the crest, Revenue drew down on him and let go. The horse dropped, the rider screamed; and then both Revenue and Salt were out of the ravine and flat on their bellies.

Once in action, Nick Salt seemed to forget he was mortal enough to be dented by lead. Rising boldly to his feet, he ran out into the prairie. "Damn you hounds, I know every one of your names and I despise the ground you crawl on! Come and get it!" Revenue followed.

The remaining three Rafter T riders started out of the black distance on a forward charge. They raced in, swinging down the lead. Revenue and Salt, standing abreast of each other, answered coolly. The plunging outlines wavered. A voice yelled, "I'm piled!" Then there were but two outlines. A man ran off awkwardly, seemed to be picked up and carried away; two farewell shots came through the weaving black. After that the drumming echoes dimmed and died and there was left only the sick groan of a man near the rim of the creek.

Revenue advanced cautiously. "Hit?" he asked.

"Horse busted my leg when he fell. Here, I'm out of this. Gimme a hand."

"Throw your gun this way," directed Revenue. "I want to hear it hit."

The man obeyed, gun falling somewhere near by. Revenue drew in and discovered the Rafter T rider propped against a dead pony. Salt struck a match and instantly whipped it out; but in the short glow the rider's dark, thick face could be seen locked in pain.

"Cahoon," muttered Salt. "Lose no sympathy on this rat, Revenue. He's tortured plenty of others. How's it feel to suffer, Cahoon?"

"Salt," gasped the man, "I'll live to get you for that talk!"

"Hits home, don't it?" jeered Salt unsympathetically. "Like all gun-fanning bullies you're yellow clear down to the white meat."

"You'll get yours!" ground out Cahoon. "No man ever tore clear of Rafter T yet and lived to tell tales."

Revenue broke in. "How long have you been with that outfit, Cahoon?"

"None of your damn business!"

"A long time," put in Salt. "He's LeGrue's left-hand man. Him and an egg by the name of Lugg. And another called 'the Badger.'"

"What's all the shooting about?" pressed Revenue. "What are you dudes trying to hide?"

"You'll never find it! Good God, are you goin' to let me stay here and suffer?"

"Listen to him squawk, Revenue."

Cahoon jerked his body upright. "What was that name!"

Revenue answered with swift intentness. "Ever hear of it before, Cahoon? Does it mean anything to you?"

But Cahoon was sullenly silent, suppressing even his display of pain. He sat tense and expectant, head thrown back, the drawn features making a pallid blur.

Revenue dropped to the ground and set an ear against it. He rose. "They're trying to play Apache on us out yonder. Creeping this way. You'll have help soon enough, Cahoon." Leaning down, he stripped the man's gunbelt free. "Come on, Salt. Time to trot."

"My regards to the bunch," jeered Salt. "Tell 'em I hope they all die sudden."

Cahoon said nothing. The partners retreated to the creek,

saddled and swung to the west, in the direction of the towering mountain outline. Behind them was a long, faint runner of light across the horizon. Day was just below the line. From the receding distance emerged three spaced shot echoes.

"He's found his gun and is signaling 'em to come in," guessed Salt. "Now, if we want to get very high up before daylight catches us, we better bust."

In complete silence they pressed on at a faster clip. The prairie continued as level as a floor during another two miles; then, without the preliminary warning of a rising bench or tilted foothill, the toe of the range was in front of them; and between two black shoulders of pine-studded rock was the maw of a trail.

Salt led in. They climbed stiffly and circuitously. A dashing mountain stream boiled down from the heights and across it rested a plank bridge which took the sound of their traveling ponies' hoofs and shot it up enormously to the sky. Dawn flushed the east, a wedge of pale violet inserted into the otherwise solemn heavens.

So, while night grudgingly gave ground and the swirling fog wreathed sluggishly from draw to peak, they climbed. Salt kept leaning forward as they rounded one overhanging rock face after another, and at each such maneuver his arm went trailing toward the butt of his gun. They came to a brief, narrow meadow across which they ran rapidly. Beyond it the throat of the trail narrowed between dismal cliff sides; but Salt, instead of accepting this route, tackled a steep climb to the right and at the end of three-quarters of an hour halted in the shelter of dwarf pines.

Day had come with a rush and a brilliance; the ponies were badly blowing. They dismounted. Salt led Revenue along an alleyway between the trees and halted at the very edge of a precipice, pointing below. "There's where we'd wound up if we had stuck to the main trail. Rafter T line cabin. Always a man in it."

Fully three hundred feet below the main trail debouched into an alpine meadow that ran irregularly between the still higher peaks to the southward. Banks of fog obscured the far end. Here and there small channels of this meadow curved around the foot of the peaks, apparently leading to other meadows beyond sight. It was a lush, grassy land, drenched by night moisture and fed by innumerable small creeks flowing off those glacial summits from which the shrouding fog had not yet lifted. Directly at the entrance to this main meadow sat a cabin with a light gleaming through a single window and a curling funnel of smoke pouring from a chimney. Even as they watched, the door of the cabin opened and a man stepped out and went around to an adjacent lean-to. When he emerged he was leading a horse.

"He'll patrol to the south now," explained Salt, "and meet a man who relieves him. This pass here is called Peepsight. Yonder one which we can't see is No-Speak. It rises right behind Rafter T. And there's your two ways of entering this country from the eastern valley. None other, unless a man wants to fall off and bust his neck."

He went back through the small timber to another vantage point. Far below them ran the prairie, filling with strong light. The sun, still below the rim, sent up long rays of blood crimson. Firehole sat in the foreground, a huddle of miniature buildings; and in the still nearer foreground a line of riders came onward at a rapid clip, turned and aimed into the Peepsight trail.

"That's them," muttered Salt. "Nobody else would be foolish enough to come on that trail. Lay this bet with yourself, Revenue. Right at this minute LeGrue's pushing all his men up here, through this pass and through No-Speak. By nine o'clock the high country will be lousy with 'em."

"Time to eat," drawled Revenue, and withdrew to a secluded stretch of pines. He emptied a burlap sack, set aside a coffee pot, a skillet, a slab of bacon and a loaf of bread. Salt built a small fire. Over it they fried their bacon and boiled their coffee and settled down to the brief meal, using the coffee pot as a cup.

"Where's the beef?" inquired Revenue.

"It drifts to the higher meadows during the hot months," said Salt. "We'll find most of it beyond that big middle peak."

"That's our next destination," murmured Revenue. "I aim personally to hogtie a few specimens and have a look."

"I been thinking about that," admitted Salt, "and reached some funny conclusions. Old Colonel Trevison runs four brands. His main one is Rafter T. His next biggest is a Split Diamond. He's also got a Wagonwheel and a Bar Window Bar, neither of which amounts to much."

Revenue lifted his suddenly interested eyes. "A Split Diamond."

"Yeah. Now consider. The Split Diamond is plastered on a lot of old stuff. Nothing under three or four years old. And he ain't using the brand no more. All new beef is burned a Rafter T. That brand carries a few old cows, but most of it is short threes and under."

For a pair of men on the dodge, these two started the morning leisurely. Cigarette smoke curled fragrantly into the glade. Salt idly stamped out the remnants of the fire. Revenue made patterns in the dirt with a match. Presently he lifted his head and Salt saw a hard, eager light animating the Texan's gray eyes.

"I'm sure interested," stated Revenue.

"Think you got a hot trail?" asked Salt casually.

"Know better when I see some of the brands."

"No time like the present to get amalgamated," decided Salt and rose.

Revenue picked up the provision sack, threw in the utensils and tied it to the saddle thongs behind the cantle. They mounted and rode to the edge of the bluff again, looking into the alpine meadow.

"What did I say?" grunted Salt. "Look there."

The file of men which earlier had entered the foot of the trail, now swung out of it and halted by the line cabin. One of the party dismounted and entered the cabin, reappearing immediately thereafter. He waved an arm; another man dropped out. The rest of the group cantered ahead.

Revenue suddenly swore. "We're a couple of fools, Salt. Let's get away from here in a hurry."

"As how?"

"That bunch ain't as fat looking as it appeared when it hit the bottom of the trail. Some of 'em has dropped off along the way. Probably they caught our tracks swinging up this way."

"A good hunch," said Salt and turned his pony, breaking into a gallop. He called over his shoulder. "And our trail is plenty deep in the wet ground. Didn't I say LeGrue was a hound for getting what he went after?"

"Off the trail!" snapped Revenue, plunging into the deeper protection of the pines. Salt followed suit and they stopped a moment. Looking back, Revenue discovered three riders suddenly top the grade and fall into the open area where Salt and himself had loitered for breakfast. In absolute silence, the two waited while the moments dragged by. No shout of discovery pursued them; they had, apparently, not been seen. So, motioning to Salt, he went on. Salt picked a way through the heavier shelter, made a wide detour and in a little while struck fair going again. Behind them was the dampened explosion of a single gunshot.

"Signal," grunted Salt. "Mister, from now on it's going to be just one damned thing after another."

"Hit for the beef," said Revenue.

The trail they pursued kept to the spine of the ridge, turning and rising and dipping with it for about two miles. At occasional intervals the weatherwise Salt pulled into the timber and so buried the mark of their progress; but the footing here was always tediously slow and in the end he reverted to the path. Now and again they approached the edge of the ridge sufficiently close to catch a view of the meadow, from which the morning's fog was rapidly rising.

The Rafter T party had split, half of it running back toward the line cabin, the other half breaking into individual riders and striking for varying parts of the upland. Revenue observed the shifting of forces carefully and concluded that the idea was to throw some kind of a rough line around the entire range. Meanwhile, his attention was diverted in other directions as well. Behind him no sound indicated that the pursuing trio of Rafter T men was drawing nearer; but twice in the course of the last mile he had heard a slight rustling of brush off to the right. And as the two of them entered an open bay he saw, a brief two hundred feet away, a figure on foot duck from one tree to another.

"Hustle out of this, Salt," he murmured.

The partner spurred faster and they reached shelter again. Without warning, Revenue pulled away from Salt and plunged off at a tangent.

A skulking man suddenly rose from the earth and faced them, both arms lifted. In a wavering, falsetto voice he called: "I'm watching the beef, Revenue. I'm riding circle tonight. They're a-resting easy."

CHAPTER 4

Revenue cried out a name in sudden and full-throated astonishment. "Rip Corbin!" Salt came plunging forward with his gun lifted, but when he saw the man on foot he let the weapon drop.

"Hell, it's the loony gent."

Revenue dropped from the saddle and went forward. "Rip —what brought you to this shape? Good God, why I—"

The man was perhaps forty-five but he looked sixty. His clothes were all ragged, his hair and beard a discolored and matted silver. His joints stuck out and his cheeks were cadaverous. Out of incredibly blue eyes shot a leering gleam. "I'm holding the herd for you, Revenue. But mark my word, you better take care. I don't trust this crew. They's too much muttering, too much whispering behind your back. Mark my word."

"Loony as a bass drum," muttered Salt. "He's been skulking the hills ever since my time. Wild as a bottle of home-made bock beer. LeGrue's been trying to catch him for years and can't lay hand on him. Damn funny we should meet up with him thisaway."

Revenue's eyes, turned abruptly on Salt, were hard and angry. "He may be loony, but he was a Revenue rider for twenty years. Rip Corbin! Great God, look at him now! Here, Rip. You remember me?"

"I know a Revenue," said Corbin. "I have worked for you Revenues half my life, but I'm telling you this, Ansel, watch out for that cook you hired at Dodge. He ain't no good. And watch out for these new men you been hiring along the trail. They ain't no good. Ever stop to wonder how it come about we been losing our old bunch of hands? I'm warning you! No good will come of it!"

"Ansel," muttered Revenue. "That was my dad's name. He thinks I'm the old man. Rip, what's the matter with this cook? What's his name?"

"You know it, don't you?" parried Corbin shrewdly. "I don't trust this LeGrue—" Suddenly his head turned against the wind and he poised as if on the verge of flight, straining to catch some sound not audible to either of the partners.

Revenue tried again. "Where's the rest of the crew, Rip?"

Corbin seemed to labor over the question, seemed to try to break down some cloudy confusion in his sorry brain. But the effort failed. Revenue could plainly discern that the man lived in the past, that his reasoning powers led him to one certain climactic and disastrous scene and there stopped.

"By the fire, plotting with LeGrue, I reckon," muttered Corbin. "You watch out—"

He never finished the sentence. In the air was a warning for him, and like a hunted animal he sprang backward, slid through a thicket of brush and disappeared.

Revenue started to pursue and was stopped by Salt's quick words. "Come on, I hear something on the trail."

Revenue ran back to his horse and swung up, cursing. "If they get the old man . . . !"

Salt was galloping forward. "Don't worry. He's dodged everybody a long time." Then he buckled down to the chore of putting the now distinctly oncoming pursuers behind.

Revenue swore again, a brief and bitter oath that lashed into the advancing morning. The sight of old Rip Corbin had revived all the memories of his younger days, had rubbed afresh the rankling, gnawing sense of tragic uncertainty surrounding his kin. And whatever suspicions he had recently developed concerning the Rafter T were now solidified beyond doubt; Corbin had spoken LeGrue's name; Corbin had, through some dim sense of responsibility, stuck close to the cattle out yonder beyond the peaks. Linking the two facts together could mean only that those cattle were in some manner a part of the mystery.

Mark Revenue was brought out of these harsh and somber speculations by the necessities of the trail. Salt was grimly in earnest now, and going forward at breakneck speed through a country badly cut up. The pines were thinning. The moraine of a high, snow-crusted peak lay across their way, its rocky, pocketed underfooting sharply dangerous, and by every rule of safety to be taken at a discreet walk; but Salt was showing the streak of iron in him and risking all on a direct route rather than swinging away into deeper country. In front of them some hundred yards was another barrier of timber. They reached it and pressed through. Salt called back. "Let 'em try to find our tracks on that rock!" The trees lasted only a short distance. Beyond this belt was another open bay, even more rugged than the first; and beyond it the fringing forest again.

Salt pressed on. Quite gradually they skirted the base of the peak. Down a narrow vista Revenue caught sight of a farther meadow and along it a scattering of cattle. Turning in the saddle, he swept the backward trail, and found no sign as yet of the Rafter T men breaking through the timber. Salt veered a little and then they were running free through the pines, branches slashing at them and dead needles falling down in a dry, irritating shower.

The horses were working up a lather, drawing deep for wind, but Salt never slackened until a good two miles of this heavy going was behind. At that juncture the trees dwindled out to the margin of a meadow that was shaped like a bowl. One edge ran against the peak, another marched westward into an ever rising country that was dark and solitary to the eye; directly in front of the partners a wooded knoll stood up from the meadow like a ship and all around it and through it cattle ranged. The partners dismounted to let the horses blow.

"What next?" inquired Salt.

"If we go out to that knoll," said Revenue, "we can have a look at the beef and still be in shelter."

"It ain't a good place to be trapped," suggested Salt.

"No," agreed Revenue. "But the Rafter T bunch ain't all scattered around yet and stationed on points of observation. It's a dead run of about two-three minutes out there. Same back. If we wait much longer we'll probably be on the dodge and won't ever get our chance."

"True facts," was Salt's laconic observation. "You and me see alike. Do things on the jump. Consider afterward. We're going to run into grief anyhow so we might as well force the play."

Revenue listened into the morning's droning silence. No sound struck up from the rear; the trailing party evidently were beating the fringe of trees along the rock barren and making cautious work of it. He looked at Salt thoughtfully; the tawny-haired man nodded. "Here's to crime," said he and swung up. Revenue followed suit.

They moved to the edge of timber and, sinking the spurs deep, shot out across the meadow on a dead run. Suddenly they were stripped and helpless. The dark corners of the surrounding trees seemed to glare at them; the silence trembled with threat. They raced past a browsing cow which, frightened by these streaking apparitions, threw up its head and bolted; the movement took hold and in the passage of seconds half a hundred cattle were careening away to the south in full stampede. Revenue swore under his breath, knowing that this sign of restlessness would sooner or later be seen and noted by Rafter T riders and its cause suspected.

But the situation could neither be helped nor long worried about. In these flashing intervals of time there were other things striking them with a greater urgency. The knoll was dead in front of them and they swept up its gentle foot with quirts aleap. Behind was no signal as yet of discovery or pursuit; but as Revenue drew abreast of Salt and they passed into the protective timber, he thought he saw a streak of movement away off to the west—a shifting of a man from one covert of the hills to another.

"Plenty of beef in here to work on," said Salt, drawing in. The flight had left him nervous and restless. He moved in the saddle, fiddled with the reins and kept swearing in soft phrases. "Get at it. I'll keep my eye peeled."

The shaded grove held a score or so of cattle that shrewdly had sought the cool here. Revenue walked his pony on their flanks. He saw the large outline of the Rafter T brand but paid little attention to it; he saw, too, a solitary Wagonwheel steer. This as well he gave only a cursory glance. But when he came upon a mature cow bearing a Split Diamond on its left barrel, he closed in and bent over. The cow moved away; Revenue followed, eyes set intently on the brand. Salt wheeled around to the south of the knoll, still swearing, and passed by. "See anything?" he demanded.

"Plenty. This is the sort of a brand Trevison sports on his old stuff, uh?"

Salt turned and came back, passing the cow a short glance. "Yeah. That's it."

"Then I'll tell you something," said Revenue softly. "It's

37

well weathered by the years and you couldn't prove anything in court by it, but that was once upon a time an Arrow cow. A Revenue Arrow. Look here. The thing works out too simple to make any mistake."

He dismounted and drew the Arrow brand in the dust, long shaft and broad head, as follows: ➤. Then he brought the points of the head diagonally to the center of the shaft and then down to join the end of it, creating this: ⬦. "There she is. That sort of a shift wouldn't get by in Texas, but up here nobody's the wiser."

"So it's stolen beef they're guarding so all-fired close?" muttered Salt, forgetting his nervousness. "That's why LeGrue patrols this range like it was full of diamonds. Split Diamonds."

"Rip Corbin gave me an idea," said Revenue. "An idea of about how they worked it. Dad started out with a good crew. Along the way some of 'em must have died and their places were filled in by others. I'd say it was a scheme worked by LeGrue aforehand with his men planted all along the trail. By and by he's got his own partners riding with the outfit and he's strong enough to kill the rest of the old Arrow boys, take over the beef and run 'em up here."

"Wholesale stealing," said Salt, struck by the enormousness of the idea. "Rustling a ranch *in toto!*"

"And wholesale killing," added Revenue, somberly. "An outfit wiped from the map and a trail herd shoved into a country where nobody knows the difference. A wild country like this. They've doctored all the Arrows over to Split Diamonds, which must have taken 'em a hell of a long time. Then as the young stuff came along it was plastered with Rafter T—and the slate is clear."

Salt was deep in thought, struggling with some idea that would not show daylight. "Yeah. That'd explain the mystery around the ranch, all right. LeGrue probably has took the road all crooks take. Killed off his confederates one by one to erase knowledge of the transaction. Didn't I say nobody was fired, but that men died accidentally in the hills? Sure. Then to fill up the gap he'd hire some sucker like you or me and keep us. The old-timers who knew about the business wasn't speaking nothing to nobody. Gradually they'd get shuffled off. Then there'd be just a bunch of riders who didn't know what the deal was. Nobody except LeGrue—and Trevison. That's what gets me. Where's Trevison come into the scene? I don't make it?"

"Ain't he the main push?" demanded Revenue. "LeGrue seems to be afraid of him."

"Hell," grunted Salt, "that always seemed like a lot of foolishness to me. Trevison's a fat, old, feeble, whining codger. He couldn't be the main push of nothing. LeGrue plays him up for some purpose, which I dunno why."

Revenue rolled a cigarette and smoked it in long, heavy draws of breath. His head was down, the gray eyes mirroring a darkness that spread like actual color across the rest of his features. Salt watched him, seeing a stranger in this Texan. The ease and drawl and loose-knitted laziness faded away and instead there was a thin-lipped fellow, all cold and quiet and emotionless.

"Well," prompted Salt, coming back to a realization of their surroundings, "now that you know the deal, what's it to be?"

Revenue said briefly, "They're dogs, damn their bloody hearts! I'm going to get 'em!"

"The old original bunch," reflected Salt, "would probably be LeGrue, Cahoon, Lugg, and a white-faced rat who calls himself the Badger. Every one of 'em a killer and no pity as ever I found. The rest are boys hired afterward, like me. Even so, they're all tough. Figure Trevison anyway you want. I don't know how to put him. All told, sixteen hands to buck."

"There's just me left, of all my family," said Revenue, very slow and bitter. "Not another soul of us left. Makes no difference if I die, which I soon enough will. But I'll settle the account before I go. We're going to run a two-man war, Salt."

"Right with you on that," said Salt.

Revenue dropped his cigarette, turned in one long, sweeping motion and sprang to the saddle. From the north came the distinct running reverberation of horses put to a hard pace. Both partners spurred to the northern fringe of trees, discovering half a dozen men advancing in a widespread formation. Those in the center of the line lagged a little while the end riders pushed farther out to circle the knoll. Salt swore and galloped to the rear. Across the distance Revenue heard him calling. "Here's where this two-man war begins serious-like. Another bunch boosting up the valley from No-Speak."

Revenue retreated and met his partner. "They've got us pegged," added the latter. "And I rise to remark it's no place to be for a duration of time."

"There's a couple holes they ain't got plugged yet," said Revenue and motioned swiftly to the west and east. "We split right here, Salt. You break for the east and ride into the timber. I'll go for the hills to the west. That'll break up their play. Meet me tonight where we cooked our breakfast

Salt was no hand to debate. He accepted the fact as p
and whirled his horse. "All right. If either of us don't mak
it there, figure to go on to the bottom of Peepsight and o
out to the creek where we camped." Then, in a wild burst of
speed, he raced his pony from the sheltered knoll and dow
the grade.

Revenue was already into the meadow on the opposit
side. Bending well over, he ventured a glance toward th
nearest group of Rafter T men. They had instantly spotte
both himself and Salt; a volley of shots exploded ragged
into the increasingly hot morning. Through the thin air ra
a strong, excited cry: "This way—this way!" And then th
bunch wheeled and went racing after Salt who had gaine
several hundred feet. It left Revenue out of danger for th
moment, but although he couldn't see Salt, he knew th
yellow-haired partner would have a close race to run befor
gaining the shelter of the pines.

Meanwhile, the other and larger party, bearing down from
the No-Speak Pass trail, was nearly within rifle shot an
seemed also to be verging after Salt. Noting that, Revenu
elected to dangle himself in front of the bunch as live ba
and so remove the extra pressure from his partner. Swinging
he laid a course across the flank of the larger party; hardl
had he done so when all the riders came impetuously aroun
in a wide deploying line and strained at him.

Since both Revenue and the Rafter T men were going fu
tilt, the danger of collision instantly presented itself. The
were driving onward at an angle that threatened to shut hir
away from the ranking trees of the western slope, graduall
maneuvering him into a position that would necessitate
long retreat to the north. Realizing this, Revenue veere
away from them, and for a space of time pursuers and pur
sued raced abreast of each other with a distance of abou
five hundred yards intervening.

Revenue hung low in the saddle, calculating his chance
coldly and finding them slim. The only piece of fortun
seemed to lie in the presence of an outthrust line of pine
coming from the slope boldly into the open meadow like
pointing finger. Once he had gained the lee of this protec
tion he knew his chances of survival would increase enor
mously, but there was even a doubt about that; for the hors
beneath him, already punished by several hard spurts durin
the morning, was perceptibly flagging, struggling for wind
smooth stride breaking into a labored chop.

Meanwhile, the pursuing party had tired of the neck-and
neck running and came around against him, essaying to catc

him short of the trees. Revenue spent a moment in lightning calculation. If he turned away from them he made the run to shelter that much the longer, and his horse was gradually losing speed. If he kept on the direct route it became a matter of doubt whether he or LeGrue's men would strike the trees first.

The most drastic measure seemed the best; he kept his course, drew out his gun and laid down a sudden barrage of bullets. He hoped, not for a direct hit, but for a break in their running. The move appeared futile. Instead of checking, the Rafter T men spurred and at the same time opened on him; and as he saw how near at hand the actual collision was, and how far—even though the distance was a matter of yards —the shelter of the trees was, he consigned himself to a measure of last resort; which was to swing and face them.

In fact, his hand actually had tightened on the reins to perform the movement when from some aperture of the trees there came a wicked, spitting rifle fire. It was rapid and sustained, and Revenue, neither feeling nor hearing the impact of shells around him, looked over to the Rafter T bunch to find it torn apart, all in confusion. Two horses were down, the rest bucking away; and then, as the pursuit momentarily quit him, Revenue ran by the arm of trees, came upon a trail that began to rise between rocky shoulders, and placed himself in temporary safety.

A crisp, feminine voice said from some covert: "This way. Hurry up."

Revenue looked vainly around him.

"Higher," said the voice with growing impatience. "Keep coming!"

He rose with the trail, ran by a mass of volcanic rubble and came upon her—a lithe, tall, grave girl standing behind a natural parapet and resting her rifle on it. Ahead of her was an alley in the greenery that gave her full view of the meadow and the Rafter T bunch. She fired another shot and suddenly handed the gun to him with a gesture of dislike. "You keep at it. Don't stop. Make 'em run or they'll kill you! I know that outfit! Hurry, make 'em run before they get into timber!"

Revenue slid from the saddle and took stand. She laid a handful of shells beside him and seized the reins of his horse, speaking soothingly at the jaded beast. Revenue began to fire. He knocked one man out of the saddle just as the whole group had collected and started on again. The shot disarranged their purpose badly. Revenue, working with a cool, grim intensity of purpose, sprayed the lead across the moderate distance. A horse fell, another man reeled and only saved himself by grasping his saddle pommel as the mount carried him beyond Revenue's sight. The rest of the riders had enough; they ran rapidly northward and so were hidden. Revenue sprang down the trail a few yards, expecting them to charge up it. But they had left the area entirely alone and were bound for some other part of the forest.

"Follow me," said the girl, running for the brush. She disappeared and came back astride a giant bay. "Hurry up! They'll swing around and be on top of us in a minute."

Revenue obeyed. The girl rode along the trail a quarter mile, left it for another, climbed the steep side of a butte and presently halted on an eminence that gave them a complete view of the meadow and surrounding hills while at the same time affording them the protection of an encircling thicket. She slipped off her horse, and Revenue for the first time had a chance to appraise her carefully.

"Who are you anyhow?" he wanted to know.

"My name is Lee Trevison, of Rafter T," said she.

CHAPTER 5

"Thunder!" said Revenue. "And those men you been pickin' off—"

"Work for Rafter T," interrupted the girl briefly.

"Now wait," went on Revenue, getting control of his astonishment. "You're the girl I saw on the ranch-house porch last night—crying."

"As I have been doing for many, many nights," put in the girl with a sad, bitter emphasis. She sat on a log, looking up at him out of eyes that seemed tragic beyond the ability ever to smile; dark gray eyes with inexpressible depths to them. She was square-shouldered and there was a quiet resolution to her poise, as if she had made up her mind and meant to abide by whatever decision made. Yet for all these marks of firmness, she was a more feminine woman than Revenue had seen in a long time. Black hair curled gracefully at her temples, and her candid features were softly pleasant.

"I don't make this," said Revenue, "but I aim to. You shot at your own men?"

"LeGrue's men," corrected the girl.

"LeGrue's your man, ain't he?"

"LeGrue is nobody's man," said the girl. "He takes no orders."

"None from your dad?" questioned Revenue.

At that a still darker, unhappier expression came to her eyes. "My poor father hasn't given an order on that ranch for two years and a half."

Revenue considered these answers and found them all at odd lengths to one another. So he tackled the problem from a different angle. "My name's Revenue," he explained.

"I know it," said Lee Trevison. "I saw you ride in yesterday. I heard you talking to LeGrue in the shadows. I saw you go to town. And I heard about you when the men came back. Both from LeGrue and later from Cahoon."

"How come you to be here?"

"I followed the bunch this morning. They don't know it, but I did. I understood what they were trying to do—which was get you and Salt. So I followed."

Revenue was a direct-minded man. He believed in cutting straight through to a given point. "What for?"

"I thought I might be able to head you off, warn you. You see what happened? I was of some help, wasn't I?"

"I rise to remark," stated Revenue with considerable warmth. The girl's face took on color; she looked away. "But," proceeded Revenue, grimly insistent, "what'd you do it for?"

"Did you ever try using your head?" parried Lee Trevison, somewhat provoked.

"I can do any amount of guessing," agreed Revenue. "Being called upon to do so, I might venture to conclude you have no sympathy with the present layout on your ranch."

The girl was a little scornful. "After seeing what I have done, I should think you might safely rely on the assumption."

But Revenue was approaching his goal flat-footedly. "It's also possible LeGrue is overstepping his authority to the extent of trying to run the ranch."

"He has controlled it exclusively since he came to us," replied the girl.

Revenue paused to roll a cigarette, eyes narrowing. Looking up, he shot a swift question at her. "Where was your dad three years ago?"

"On the ranch, minding his own business," said the girl with frowning emotion. "We had one of the finest outfits in this country. We were doing nicely. We were minding our own business and living as Christian people should live. Now —now look. We're prisoners—no other way to put it!"

Revenue nodded, reaching some sort of a conclusion. "So LeGrue came to your place about two and a half years ago with a tough outfit and five thousand head of beef. He forced your dad to take him as partner on the crooked deal. And he's been lording it ever since."

"How do you know all that?" demanded Lee Trevison, startled.

"Because that beef belonged to the Revenue family once," was the Texan's curt reply. "LeGrue butchered my dad's outfit somewhere on the trail and lifted the whole works."

"I knew you weren't just a puncher when you rode into our yard!" cried the girl, her face changing queerly.

A few sputtering shots came rolling up the slope. Revenue ran to the edge of the bluff, parted the brush and looked out upon a meadow filling with heat haze. The shots had emerged from his left, probably from some area near the trail over which he had recently fled. Nothing was to be seen there now; but in the direction of the Peepsight trail a party of men were forming and moving—advancing down the valley toward the No-Speak end.

"Do you see now why I came here this morning?" challenged the girl. "You will never be able to understand the torture and misery and fear there is in it for Dad and me. To live on a ranch that is yours, but yet is robbed from you! To stand by and see a group of the blackest kind of cutthroats filling the yard day by day. To hear their insults and taunts! To know that they have killed others almost under your eyes, as I know it. And never any hope of getting away. Not for a minute. LeGrue watches us like hawks. We are not free. It is only because he is so set on having you and Salt that he relaxed his vigilance today."

"How about other men in the valley?" put in Revenue. "Or other outfits? Nobody ready to take care of you?"

"Some men believe my father to be a party to LeGrue's treachery and violence. Others know better but are afraid. Don't you understand? LeGrue lets nobody onto our range and very few inside our gate. People of the country realize that, even though they don't know the story of the stolen cattle. They think LeGrue rustles. He lets them think it. And they don't dare interfere, for he is a cold-blooded killer. So I have stood by, watching my father grieve and go to pieces; and hoping a man would come along. A man!"

Revenue's attention snapped back to the party sweeping across the meadow. It ran abreast of the high point on which himself and the girl were hidden; and over the distance he saw something in the formation that puzzled him and woke a cold apprehension. The riders were two abreast excepting for the front file. There, three men went shoulder to shoulder and the middle man had his hat off. He seemed to be clutching the pommel, for his hands never lifted, and from time to time he swayed uncertainly in the saddle, upon which the adjoining riders appeared to press in. Suddenly Revenue ripped out an oath.

"They've got Salt!"

The girl ran beside him, shielding her eyes against the sun. "I recognize him. Yes. And they're taking him back to the ranch. I know what that means!"

Revenue's cheeks were dark and hard. Swift cruelty came to his mouth. "What does it mean?"

"That they will torture him for information about you, extort everything he has revealed about the ranch. Then tonight they'll take him into the hills—and kill him!"

Revenue stood like stone until the cavalcade was well beyond and turning for a straighter approach to the throat of No-Speak. He swung on the girl then and motioned her back. "Get to your horse and ride home before they reach it."

"What are you going to do?"

"Settle with LeGrue."

A quick sigh escaped her. "Do you know how utterly bad he is? Do you know—"

"It's the same old story," interrupted Revenue. "The story of a killer running riot. Still, I mean to settle. Go home. See where they put Salt and how they have him corralled. Get an extra gun. Tonight after dark I'll crawl down there. Meet me—" He paused, trying to visualize the layout of the ranch yard. "Meet me behind your main house."

"Have you an idea . . . ?"

He shook his head. "Not even the whiskers of an idea. But I'll be there. Go on now."

She climbed into the saddle and looked down at him, thoughtful, reserved and with the flicker of an emotion in her eyes he could not name. The beating sun began to bead up the sweat on his forehead and he removed his hat; a stray lock of hair fell awry and at the moment he looked like a boy puzzled and angered and uncertain. She rode near him and laid a hand on his shoulder.

"I have prayed for a man," said she quietly, "and I think the prayer is answered. I am afraid—for LeGrue is like terror. But—I am glad to know you are here. Be very careful, please." Then she lifted her arm in farewell and ran through the brush to timber.

Revenue sat on a rock and watched the meadow. Near noon he found a cold lunch out of his gunnysack; in midafternoon he thought he discovered men stealing across a higher level—and at the warning he shifted location. Later, another party ran up from No-Speak and headed directly for Peepsight trail; and for a little while the meadow was filled with patrols rounding from one section to another. Then the sun went down, twilight tarried a brief moment and disappeared. It was dark. Revenue, moving with that extreme and methodical deliberation of a man who has weighed his chances, mentally written off his career and closed his mind to whatever hurt and misfortune might be ahead, got on his horse and turned down to the meadow, bound for the trail through No-Speak and the Rafter T Ranch.

Mark Revenue still had no plan, other than to take a straight and strict course toward the ranch. Night had arrived and he knew that if LeGrue meant to settle with Salt, it would be in this same dark. So, to aim through the open meadow and take his chances at the pass was the only thing to do. Once at the ranch, his affairs were in the lap of the gods. He had a duty to perform that transcended all other obligations and desires, which was to rescue his partner—that partner whom he had known for only twenty-four hours, but nevertheless a man who had thrown in with him, share and share alike. And such was his training, such was his implicit obedience to the elemental rules of an elemental land that he did not even debate the proposition, did not even admit of an existing alternative.

He arrived at the meadow and went across it at a free run, the sound of hoofs and the squealing of gear rising and vanishing into the thin, crispy cold air. The heavens were laced with dim stars, the roundabout ridges and peaks blackly etched against a lesser black. Somewhere other riders were questing the meadows and he believed the throat of No-Speak would be guarded; but still he pressed on, guided by the clearly outlined notch to the fore. Nor did he think of what lay before him. Rather he felt the rhythm and solitude of a world asleep, the call of the deep primeval land. So he entered the shoulders of No-Speak, tended downward and was without warning challenged by someone standing behind a black boulder.

"Who's there?"

The man was hidden a hundred feet on Revenue's mind leaped alive, absorbing the possibilities of the situation. There were other Rafter T men still in the meadow; this guard might well be expecting some of them to come through the pass. So, drawing his gun and letting it lie along one leg, he kept his pace until the guard moved from the protection of the rock and confronted him five yards away. Revenue made a feint at familiarity. "That you, Badger?"

"Hold on there," said the guard, curt and forbidding.

46

"Don't you know the rules of this game yet? Badger's below, as you ought to be aware. Who is it?"

Revenue turned to another expedient, understanding he would never get by unchallenged. He tightened the reins and ripped the pony with his spurs; the beast bucked onward in rebellion. Revenue said, "Confound you, stand still! Come around—head up and stop that pitching!" Meanwhile, the pressure of his body guided the pony on until it slid abreast of the guard.

That one, wary and unconvinced, jerked the head of his horse away, ripping out another warning. "Hold your animal!" Revenue used his spurs again and set the pony dead against the other. His gun rose and crashed down on the guard's flaring stetson. The man was done for and pitched to the ground with a belch of wind. Revenue seized the riderless pony at the bit and held him, swiftly considering.

"It's a long game, not a short one. This man won't sleep more'n five minutes. He's got to be out of the way."

He tied the reins of the guard's pony to the pommel of his own horse, dismounted and unbuckled the man's gunbelt. He stripped the man's boots off, threw them into the brush. He took his rope, made two stiff ties at the guard's arms and feet and threw in a brace of back-breaking hitches. Then he dragged his burden down the slope of the mountainside fifty feet, propped him to a tree and made another tie. Lastly, he passed his hands along the rocky surface until he found a stone that, with pressure, went inside the man's mouth. This he secured with his own neckpiece, drawn from teeth to neck and knotted. Then he ran back up the slope, appropriated the gunbelt, mounted and went on with the extra horse trailing behind. There was a prickle of sweat along his skin.

"If the man squeals he'll gag, and if he gags he'll choke. One try and he'll sit tight. Now if there's another—"

Rounding a turn of the trail, Mark Revenue saw the lights of the ranch winking below, apparently so directly below that a tossed stone would have gone through a roof. Keeping on, he marked the location of the lights and by them identified the main house and the string of lesser structures leading away from the yard to the front gate. At the same time he cast up accounts. Sixteen men comprised the crew. Of these, Cahoon was laid up, the guard put away. Another pair must have been hit in the sniping at the meadow early that morning and consequently were more or less out of order. Four from sixteen left twelve. His judgment told him that at least another four were cruising the meadow, leaving eight to be accounted for. And as he reached that total there

47

came to his mind Nick Salt's statement: "They're all bad but the four old original members of the bunch are worst. That's LeGrue, Cahoon, Lugg and a rat-faced kid called the Badger."

And unless his estimate of human nature erred, he knew that those four would be somewhere inside the Rafter T compound now, working on Salt.

The trail let down with greater pitch. Revenue checked his pony to a slow walk, trying to soften the click of shod hoofs on rock. Another few feet and that worry left him, for the hard underfooting gave way to the soft alluvial of the valley. From that point on he had an open course, to right or left or directly ahead. Inborn caution took him semi-circularly away from the mouth of the trail. Deep in the gloom of a poplar cluster he dismounted, buckled the captured gunbelt around him and left the ponies. Half on his knees and half upright he returned to the trail for bearings, calculated the ground ahead of him a long moment, sidled toward the house and came within whispering distance of the rear door. Flat on his stomach he suddenly thought of a source of trouble hitherto unplanned for—the pack of Rafter T hounds.

But as the dragging, ever tightening minutes went by, nothing came of that worry. The dogs were mute, as also seemed to be all other animate sources of sound. A strange, depressing, brooding calm rested throughout the shadows, broken only by the trickle of water, the washing echo of wind in the tree tops, the irregular stuttering of a hydraulic ram. The back door was closed; no lights were visible from the windows facing him; and after an interminable quarter hour had passed he knew for a certainty the girl was not keeping the rendezvous. Somehow his plans had gone awry.

Little things bothered Mark Revenue; the beat of his heart, small and regular, against the damp earth; the bite of the air through his thin clothes; and phantom shapes that drew his wary eyes and tightened his nerves, to presently dissolve. The first tangible evidence he received of human occupancy hereabouts was the scrape of a chair on some far porch.

Then, on the heels of that sound there came the sharp striking of many hoofs on the No-Speak trail. A party filed down, passed within twenty yards of him and went around to the compound. Revenue counted five shapes against the velvet backdrop of the night. A murmur of voices reached him, indistinguishable but swift and to the point. Afterward two men ran back afoot and halted at the mouth of the trail. One said, "Right here and don't move. Keep it blocked." The other returned to the compound.

Mark Revenue knew then he had walked into a trap.

He remained quite still on his stomach, one thumb working a trench in the sandy earth, slowly lifting certain sure facts out of the flood of impressions racing through his mind. This was LeGrue's handiwork. The killer knew the ways of men. He owned an animal wisdom. He understood that even as mated beasts fought for each other, so would one partner return to rescue another. And with this knowledge he coldly placed his pawns. It meant something that the girl failed to appear; it meant something that a guard was now stationed at the foot of the trail. Considering this move, Revenue decided the returning patrol had either found the trussed and gagged man or made a good guess as to the reason for his disappearance.

It would not do to wait longer for the girl. Each moment of spending time swung the advantage more and more to LeGrue. So thinking, Revenue dragged himself to the corner of the house, out from it to the piled-up layers of shadow beside a shed, and onward to one wall of the barn. From that location he commanded the compound, the crew houses, the porch of the main house and a partial view of the small street running down to the gate.

A beam of light pressed through the main house door and cut a yellow shaft half across the yard. Against its radiance he saw two people sitting on the porch. He recognized them immediately—Lee Trevison and her father. They were still, too still; the girl sat rigidly upright, the man was slumped over and seemed ready to collapse. These were attitudes of strain and they told a story to Revenue that set his glance to roving around the compound. In an obscure corner by one of the bunkhouses he found a figure almost merged with the blackness. Then he knew.

"Forcing 'em to stay there," said Revenue to himself. "For bait."

He crept to the corner of the barn and drew back after a single look. A man there, too, half in and half out of the barn opening. Somebody came along the street and started to cross the compound. A sibilant, savage command fell on him like the crack of a whip. "Back—damn you, back!" The fellow recoiled from sight. Thoroughly aroused, Revenue crawled to the rear of the barn and halted. He could not determine if there were men waiting here but he suspected the fact and so, laboriously, he swung wide of the barn and settled to a steady progression along a line of sheds.

He had no idea where they were keeping Salt, but he believed the bunkhouses to be the best bet and accordingly he concluded to continue the weary circle around the Rafter T quarters and thus reach them. Meanwhile, the compressed silence began to play on his nerves. He had come to believe that LeGrue figured him to be already within the limits of the yard—the arrangement of men indicated it, the plain and unmistakable feeling of expectancy pervading the place indicated it. And under such circumstances every stirring of hoof, every scuttling murmur of barn rat, every near and remote whining of loose boards became a threat. The break would come, Revenue knew that. At some point or another he would run into the set jaws of the trap. The odds were against him.

At that juncture, pressed against the long wall of some building which adjoined the ranch street and with his body half risen, Mark Revenue suddenly compressed his muscles and stopped. Inside that building was the mutter of a heavy, angry voice and following it the much thinner tone of another man replying. There was no window here, but a crack in the boards let out a slice of light and just beyond it lay a kind of alley between structures. The voices rose.

"So you blabbed? We'll kill that gent before the night's over."

"Go to hell," said the thinner voice, and Revenue recognized it then. Salt was speaking.

"You'll go first, you yellow rat!"

Afterward was the dead flat echo of a palm striking flesh. Salt cried, "Lugg, I'll live to pay off!"

A barren laugh ran out of the place. Revenue collapsed to his stomach and crawled through the blade of light, coming to the alley. He entered it and saw the dark slash of the ranch street twenty feet on. Beside him was another aperture in the flimsy wall through which lamp-glow dimly seeped. Throwing himself around he placed his eyes against the crack and saw the boots of one man roaming back and forth, appearing and disappearing. That was all. Salt was apparently secured in some other part of the place.

Revenue drew back and left the alley by the same way he had entered. He retraced his toilsome route along the back walls of the buildings, crossed an open space and with infinite caution approached the rear of the barn. An intensely black rectangle appeared, and he judged it to be an open door. Near it he rested and watched.

But not for long. The thing Revenue worst feared now happened with an unexpectedness that hit him like a bullet. Over on the far side of the ranch rose the brawling, eager bay of the hound pack suddenly released and put on scent. And in the space of time it took Mark Revenue to be aware of that danger, the pack had gone back toward the mouth of the No-Speak trail, lifted his scent and started to pursue it in full throat.

Revenue could not longer be cautious. Rising, he ran inside the barn, turned against the foot of an enormous hay pile and whipped out a match. He put his body against the light, dropped it in the hay and tarried a moment to watch it catch and rise. After that he ducked out of the barn and boldly raced toward the building in which he had heard Salt. When he came to it he turned down the small alley and stopped just short of the ranch street. The hounds, momentarily confused by the vagaries of his trail, were spilling into the compound and yapping at the sides of the barn. A little later they seemed to catch the scent again for Revenue heard the nearing and swelling of their uproar. Above it rose the high, excited yell of a man. "Fire! Hey, LeGrue—fire! Fire in the barn!"

Revenue crouched in his covert. A pair of men ran by him, coming from the front gate. The ranch bell clanged. Then the door of the near building opened and Salt's captor sprang out and also raced toward the compound without a backward glance. Revenue slid by the corner with his gun raised, reached the door and flung himself inside. A lantern stood on a table, a chair lay overturned on the floor and bound to it was Salt, yellow hair streaked and clotted with his own blood. His face made a white blur and his eyes were gleaming strangely; but when he saw Revenue a small and familiar grin broke across his pinched, pained face.

"Almost too late for the wedding," he grunted.

Revenue whipped out his knife and slashed the binding rope. Salt stood up and squinted with the hurt of his muscles. Revenue passed him the extra belt and gun. "Able to make it?" he demanded.

"I'm in a humor to fight even if I had two busted legs," jerked out Salt. "You set that fire, uh?"

"Come on," snapped Revenue. He turned down the lantern wick and paused at the door. The dogs were off by the barn again, apparently abandoning the scent in favor of the fire which had begun to produce a steady, sucking roar. Broadening crimson light shuttered over the housetops, and by its glow Revenue saw men hurrying across the compound with buckets, dripping blankets, broken tree limbs. A small explosion shook the earth; a bunch of horses stampeded down the narrow street.

Salt ran ahead of Revenue with a suppressed, nervous murmur. "I know a place. Come on." He crossed the street and ran into a shed. A door let them out the back side. They turned here, paralleled the bunkhouses and halted. The whole scene was open to them, the compound and burning barn in front, main house to the left. And over everything lay the flickering blood-glow of the fire that stormed and roared inside the tinder-dry shell of boards. The Rafter T crew moved around it in confusion. Somebody held a hose and played a jet of pulsing water ineffectually along the walls. Salt started forward.

"Hold on," warned Revenue.

"Now's the time—"

"May be other men back of us," Revenue cautioned. "Le-Grue's too slick—"

"*LeGrue!*" a new voice called out.

Both men whirled to the right. Cahoon stood framed in the bunkhouse door beside them; he steadied himself on one good foot and lifted a gun, sighting it deliberately against Salt. And down the length of the muzzle, at that moment, Revenue, already swinging aside and drawing, saw a face black and heavy and brutal with lips crawling up from yellow teeth. Salt was off balance, his arm moved slowly, and so it was Revenue who fired at Cahoon, the forty-five slug striking the man and sending him spinning back into the bunkhouse. Even then there was power enough left in him to yell again, "LeGrue," and power enough to move. Cahoon crawled back through the door, lifted a malignant glance on the man he had tried to kill, and fell senseless.

Both partners were drawing aside into the shadows behind the bunkhouse. Cahoon's cry had warned the Rafter T bunch, had penetrated the soughing roar of the flames; and to a man they turned, stared and split across the compound for shelter. LeGrue alone stood his ground, moving from obscurity to the full brightness of the area. His full-throated yell rang along the walls. "Come out here! Rush 'em! Bust into 'em! Come out here!"

"Get him!" snapped Salt. "I'll watch this other—"

"Save your lead," grunted Revenue. "They're too far off. Keep your eyes peeled. They'll try to flank us—"

LeGrue's slight, whiplike body swayed. His back was to the flames and the crimson glow cast a dark, saturnine spot on his cheeks. He had not yet drawn. Rather, he stood still, arrogant and cruelly confident; and, as if to enjoy to the full the despair and defeat of his victim before the final kill, he sent a taunting, vindictive call over the compound. "Revenue—you're the last of the tribe and you'll go down like the rest did!"

"So you were the cook?" challenged Revenue, stepping into view.

"I was the cook," said LeGrue. "And I cooked 'em a good meal before they went to slaughter!"

Revenue turned to flame and fury. "LeGrue!"

LeGrue laughed sardonically. "Some died at Dodge. One went at Ogallala. The rest out on the trail, never knowing what hit 'em! Your dad and kid brothers are in the high hills, Revenue, and their bones picked clean a long time ago!"

Out of the shadows moved another man, tall and thin and forbidding. He wheeled beside LeGrue with a kind of grim carelessness. And he spoke to the foreman sharply. "You talk too much, Al. Shut your mouth and come on." The two of them fell in step and marched forward, guns lifting.

Salt ran back from the side of the bunkhouse a moment, saw the scene and cried, "Lugg, damn his heart! He's another butcher! Now where's the Badger!"

Revenue waited stolidly for the distance to shorten. The lead from the guns of these two implacable, bloody men began to rip through the wood of the bunkhouse wall, and then they passed the invisible mark that Revenue had set. Throwing his weapon forward, Revenue began to fire. And as he stepped even further out from the protection of the bunkhouse door, expecting a hail of lead from LeGrue's men but ready to meet the inevitable, something happened beyond his power to imagine.

From the far shadows a voice called out: "LeGrue, you and Lugg will fight this out alone. We're finished, you dirty dog!" LeGrue halted, surprised, and in that instant of hesitation Revenue's gun spat a pellet of lead true and straight to the murderer's heart. LeGrue clutched at his breast, turned to one side and fell, already stiff with death.

Lugg squared himself, cursed the treachery of the Rafter T riders who snarled defiance from the shadows, and pressed forward to where Revenue crouched, slipping fresh cartridges into the chamber of his six-gun. LeGrue was down, finished, but Lugg went on, stiff and formidable and brazenly unafraid. He got in a shot at Revenue before a blast from Salt's gun sent him spinning. He was done for then, and he knew it; but with a gesture only a man of iron could make, he turned completely about, raised his gun and threw it at those who had betrayed him; and then he collapsed. The roof of the barn crashed down into the caldron of flames, and the bright light flickered on the bodies of the two renegades who had been left to a just fate by those they had tricked and cursed and beaten.

Salt, watching the rear, suddenly cried, "The Badger!" Revenue flattened himself against the wall as lead beat into the boards. Salt was replying. A man screamed. Salt was running forward. Revenue swung about and saw a figure lying beneath the clump of poplar trees. Salt fired again and, still unsatisfied, spent a third shot. When he swung about his face was white as chalk. "It ain't enough," he rasped. "He had no damned right to die so sudden!"

Above the uproar of the fire sailed a voice. "You two guys! Never mind! We're finished! We don't want you! Hold your fire!"

"A trick," muttered Revenue. "We'll get into those poplars and see this thing out."

"I ain't sure," said Salt. "They're hard and they're crooked. But LeGrue treated 'em like dogs. So they didn't come to his help—and I ain't sure but what that's the end of the play."

Suddenly the rest of the Rafter T outfit swung into the compound mounted. They whirled to a brief halt. Again a spokesman's voice hailed them. "Don't be bashful, you buzzards! We're through and we're leaving for other parts! We ain't holding the sack for nobody! What's left of this joint's yours and we hope she burns to the mudsills!"

They galloped down the street, leaving behind the crackle of unleashed gunplay. Revenue ran toward the house and when he reached the porch he saw the outfit streaming through the gate. He called to Salt. "Better turn the corral stock loose and let 'em drift! This place is gone! Find a wagon —we'll have to move the Trevisons out in a hustle!"

When he turned back he saw them in the doorway waiting for him. It was his first sight of old man Trevison and he was shocked at the lined and haggard face. Trevison shook like he had the palsy. Tears rolled down his cheeks. He stretched out a hand. "My boy—you have taken me out of hell!" The girl's head was lifted, her mouth pressing back a cry.

"No time to talk about it now," said Revenue. "Better get your valuables out of here. We can't save the building."

"Let it go!" said Trevison. "It's all fouled up with the mark of those men!"

"We-ell," mused Revenue more practically, "a building is a building and takes time to put up. But these are sure gone and we'd better figure to camp in Firehole."

Trevison sank into a near chair, helpless. Suddenly the girl's grave eyes lighted and she ran into the house. Revenue followed as far as the living room. An old trunk stood in the corner, toward which she pointed. "Anything we have worth saving is there. I've kept it packed for two years."

"That all?" demanded Revenue.

"There is nothing more," said the girl. "Nothing but a happiness so great it is like a hurt. What am I to say to you?"

Revenue lifted the trunk on his arched back and carried it to the porch. Salt had found a wagon and two saddled horses. The heat began to raise blisters along the porch paint. Together the partners pulled the wagon around and loaded the trunk on it. Revenue dismounted the wagon tongue and snubbed his rope from the front axle of the vehicle to the saddle horn of one of the ponies. Salt got the idea and did likewise with the other horse.

"Time to go," said Revenue to the girl, and held out a hand. She stepped up to the seat. Trevison followed painfully. And then Revenue and Salt each climbed into a saddle, clucked to their ponies, and the animals moved off, bumping the wagon along behind.

"Revenue, forget the words I said when you first came to the outfit," Trevison said as they went along. "LeGrue used me like a tool. It was his pleasure to make a fool out of me, to play me up as a hard man. I could do nothing else than accept. The penalty for not accepting was something I will not mention." His eyes turned to the girl and Revenue caught the unspoken sentence. "But," continued Trevison, "three quarters of all the stock on my range is rightfully yours. Rafter T is mostly your outfit now. I can be only a minor partner. And, being an old man, about used up, I'm content to let it be so. You'll have to run the ranch. It's a good one, my boy."

The horses pitched restlessly and moved forward of their own accord into the poplars. Revenue turned around in the saddle and cleared his throat. "Suitable to me. I like the country, I like the situation." He looked up to the girl and found her eyes steady. It seemed to fix some inner thought. He turned to Salt. "If you were foreman, Nick, how many good riders could you get tomorrow?"

"Ample," said Salt. "Not only get 'em but keep 'em. And anybody that tries to rustle this range gets a shot in the neck. LeGrue had the right idea."

Revenue smiled slightly. "Then hop at it. And what's the use of deserting this place for Firehole? Maybe we can save a building to live in."

The girl nodded. "If you stay so will I."

Revenue got down from his horse and offered his arm to her. "That settles it. We stay." She dropped to the ground beside him and they watched the flames burning away at a corner of the main house. "Hate to see it go," was Revenue's regretful phrase. "But listen, Lee. When the ashes are cold we'll build the finest ranch house in cattleland. Heavy walls to keep the cold out in winter; high ceilings to keep the heat out of a summer."

"I'd like that," said Lee Trevison; and that was the sum and substance of their agreement. Revenue bent a glance on Salt. "What you are hanging around for? Your pay starts now. Get busy and earn it. In the morning we've got to find old Rip Corbin. He's due for a soft berth around here."

Salt walked off muttering, "Another slave driver, just like LeGrue." He threw a grin over his shoulder. Revenue winked.

The girl's hand was resting on Revenue's arm and she was saying, "A clean sweep and a happy beginning."

INVITATION
BY BULLET

CHAPTER 1

There was rain over in the distant hills. November's clouds, scudding along the ceiling of the desert, were ripped wide by the jagged peaks and emptied of their liquid freight. The immediate foreground, too, had been touched by rain; the clay-and-sand ground was sodden, every depression of hoof and pad was carved clear and every rock bowl held water. Dampness weighted the air, the raw dampness of a swiftly approaching wet winter. It was high time for all wayfarers to be holing up, yet Indigo Bowers and Joe Breedlove still were on the roll, weatherworn and scarred veterans with a thousand miles behind them and no visible goal ahead.

These two were like work ponies turned out. They found the freedom good and they tarried at green pastures only for a night, avoiding all entangling fences, refusing every bait that led to a corral. Either, left to himself and to his primal impulses, would have obeyed the sure and certain instinct of range creatures to seek shelter at this season. But together they defied rules. Shelter meant settling in town or on a ranch. It meant gathering with other men. And there would be ties and associations surely binding them during the severe months; old habits conquering the impulse to roam. And when spring came it was entirely possible that the partnership would be disrupted and only one would follow the trail again.

Neither Joe nor Indigo confessed this fear but it was very strong and real to each. Thus they rode beyond good weather, fearing to mention the need of pegging down a picket.

Indigo eased himself in the saddle and pointed his thin, waspish face into the wind. The gentleman's gross weight tallied not much more than a hundred and twenty pounds, which was wholly inadequate to withstand the wear and tear of his enormous distrust and suspicion of the universe as well as all and sundry humans moving about it. He was short and very thin and never smiled; never, in fact, found anything worth smiling at. To Indigo the world was a snare and a delusion and life was one vast effort at maintaining a proper respect for his dignity. Every day was just another twenty-four hours of possible disaster. He stared into the remote grayness of the desert, eyes contracting. And he nodded several times, moving his free arm with a gesture that his partner knew to be the forerunner of an ominous and gloomy prediction.

"I tell you, Joe, I ain't a man to go out of my way to find trouble, but this doggone' country sure gets on my nerves. The cards don't lay right whatsoever. Peril and strife is due to break down on us like a ton of bricks. Did you hear something sneaking around our camp last night?"

"Sagebrush rustling," murmured Joe.

Indigo sighed. "Joe, I ain't never ceased to marvel how you reached this ripe stage of maturity sound and unhalted. You're as innocent as a babe in three-cornered overalls. Sagebrush, eh? First time ever I heard sagebrush stumbling over rocks."

Joe smiled, a slow and crinkling smile that was like throwing wide the doors of a warm and glowing house. Joe was a tall and muscular man with silvering hair and blue eyes. He was a lazy-moving man, he spoke slowly and with a drawling gentleness, a trick that was even more pronounced when he became thoroughly roused. But even without action or speech the character of Joe Breedlove was plainly to be seen upon the fine, bronzed features—an even, humorous serenity that inevitably drew others to him. On the long trail of his life were a thousand friends who had said good-by to him with a sharp and personal sense of regret. For Joe could not walk among his kind without creating affection and respect.

"Let it pass," said he, still smiling at his peppery consort. "You been at peace with the world for a week straight and the monotony is sort of making you nervous."

"You can't slink it off thataway," grumbled Indigo, rubbing his peaked nose. "Tell me a time when I ain't been right about this feeling."

"It's a fact," admitted Joe. "I believe you could walk inside the pearly gates and drum up friction. They's something about you which makes the buzzards rise off the topmost crags and shout for a meal. Indigo, I figure you send out waves of irritation or something like that. You'd ought to be more calm. Why go out of your way to step on somebody's bunion?"

"I don't," was Indigo's severe answer. "I mind my own business strictly. But folks always got a notion they can tromp on me unrestrained. Which is sure wrong. It sure is. You talk about being calm—hell! What's it brought you? Seems like you get into trouble jusasame."

Joe swept the horizon with a long and raking glance and for an instant his attention tarried on a certain point. His smile broadened. He shook his head as if his conviction had

60

been maintained. "My motto is peace. A soft word goes a long, long ways, Indigo."

"Yeah," grunted Indigo, and stopped. His sharp eyes likewise sought the horizon, and his small body stiffened, much as a pointer freezes on quarry. Joe chuckled and rolled a cigarette.

"Somebody coming in a sweat," muttered Indigo. And for many minutes he watched the distance with jealous attention. A rider drew out of the gray air, galloping post-haste. He bore directly toward the partners for several hundred yards, then veered almost at right angles and swept upward to higher ground. Presently he was abreast of them but a half mile on their flank. And in a little while more he dropped from sight.

Indigo nodded. "Avoided us," said he with a grim satisfaction.

"Which is his right," suggested Joe.

"It ain't natural, though," argued Indigo. "It's impolite. They's a reason behind that, you wait and see."

They went on at a leisurely gait. The day was half gone and they had no exact idea where the next town lay or where they would tarry the ensuing night. It didn't much matter. They had been going on like this for a long summer. Rolling leagues of sand and sharp mountain ranges rose in front of them, were traversed and left behind. The days fell endlessly into each other. Hot, sultry days and cold, clear nights with the mystery of the infinite for a lullaby.

Joe's mellow character was in tune with all this. Cross-legged before the evening's fire he watched the blue tent of heaven and in the long silences he drew out of his memory those relics of the past which were now aged and precious. Joe was not much more than thirty-five but he had traveled the wide West from early boyhood and down that far trail were green spots with their treasured recollections. Of the night in Abilene when he had won his spurs as a man; of a girl just across the threshold of womanhood who looked up to him in the faint moonlight and cried. At this point Joe looked to the stars and his features always settled a little.

"Hah," muttered Indigo with a kind of strangled pleasure. "Another gent dusting his pants."

The second rider moved with about the same speed as the first had done, but he closed the distance with no attempt at shying away. The partners came to a standstill, waiting. Indigo shifted nervously and there was a hardening of his cheek muscles that surely and completely told of the battle chant rising within his small and skinny frame. He had been weary and jaded and morose all the morning. Now he freshened and sat erect in his saddle. Joe chuckled again, shrewdly studying the newcomer.

The rider flung himself directly in front of the partners and brought his pony to a squatting, sliding halt. He pushed back his hat with a fretful jerk and he hauled out his cigarette ingredients with the same petulance of spirit. And with the sack of makings dangling between a set of hard white teeth he stabbed the two with a flashing glance. He was youthful looking but in no manner innocent; and his bronzed face needed washing.

"Fire or disaster over yonder?" grunted Indigo. "Sudden demise, epidemical disease, peril on human hoof, or wrath of God? Or was you just limbering up the hoss?"

"If," countered the newcomer, completing the masonry of his cigarette with a sidewise slap of his tongue, "that is the only direction you boys is able to go, it is just too bad."

"Ain't the climate salubrious?" pressed Indigo, growing brighter.

The rider lit his cigarette, inhaled a mighty volume of smoke and delivered himself of a solemn sermon. "If that valley from which I just took myself hence was the vale of Eden I wouldn't go back. If there was a Persian maid every square yard to annoint my blistered spirit with kind words and loving emoluments, if there was melons on every sage bush and a pot of gold hanging from each and sundry juniper tree, if all cow critters gave milk and said milk when sparingly partook of give a gent everlasting life, I wouldn't go back. Boys, I'm on my way."

He touched his spurs and boosted his horse around them. Indigo cried after him, "Hey, what's so doggone' turrible about it?"

The rider flung a phrase over his shoulder. "Dead Card John is on the warpath." And he was gone, seeming to push the earth faster around its axis with each surge of his pony's flying feet.

Indigo blew a mighty blast from his nose and looked toward Joe with a sinister triumph. "Ain't I been telling you?"

"Making allowances for a youthful imagination—" began Joe mildly.

Indigo interrupted with one of his rare classical similes. "Once when I was a boy I used to see a picture in a book of all the animals fleeing from the Flood. Reminds me of that now. Joe, they's a heap of trouble ahead of us. Let's go a mite faster."

"It ain't our trouble," said Joe. They broke into a canter, with Indigo now and then rising in his saddle to scan the gray afternoon. "Listen, Indigo, it ain't no trouble we got to buy or share."

"Well," was Indigo's defensive answer, "I just want to look in."

The broken desert fell behind. To either side the parallel benches marched up and down and gradually sank with a falling slope. Some sort of a valley lay in the immediate foreground. Far away was the dim outline of high, sharp peaks. And Joe Breedlove, who all this time had been sweeping the earth, murmured softly and drew his horse to a complete stop. The sand to one side was scuffed with the print of hoof and human shoe. And with the outline of some heavy object dragged along its surface. Joe slid from the saddle, first spending a moment's watchfulness toward a strip of lava rock a hundred yards farther aside. "Just sort of keep your eyes on that rock," he muttered to Indigo, and bent over the broken sand.

There was a story written tragically on that area of earth. A horse had trotted back and forth, another horse had advanced into the disturbed circle and then gone off at a tangent. Two sets of boot tracks, one imperceptibly larger than the other; the gouge of knee and elbow and, ten feet from these tell-tale marks, the broad and deep trail of a dragged body. All this was elementary reading to Joe. He saw it immediately; his gloved finger dropped to a darkened patch in the sand.

"That's somebody's blood, Indigo. Let's have a look over behind them rocks."

He stepped into the saddle. And out of ingrained wariness, the pair of them split and quartered upon the rock from different angles, closing again when they had a clear view of what lay beyond. Indigo was somewhat impatient. The horizon drew him like a magnet and he waited, not bothering to get down, while Joe sought stolidly from one rock barricade to another.

"Why waste time?" Indigo demanded. "This ain't nothing. Tracks is six hours old anyhow. The main event's on ahead. Come on, Joe."

Joe's shoulders dropped. He boosted himself upright, holding a shell between thumb and forefinger. "The guy doing the shooting squatted right here, Indigo. And he must've figured he hadn't killed his man with the first shot for he ejected this shell and got set for another aim." He studied the shell with minute interest. "You wasn't in the Spanish-American War, was you, Indigo?"

"No," grunted the small partner. "I had a Spanish-American girl down at Yuma them days and that was enough fighting for one year."

"I shouldered a Krag-Jorgensen rifle during said scrap," mused Joe. "This is a sure-enough Krag shell. They ain't too common now. I guess we'll store this in a pocket."

"Let's go. They's a house two-three miles below."

They went on, Indigo's eyes growing narrower and narrower with smoldering excitement. Joe, on the other hand, was in a profound study, head dropped forward on his chest. He had just finished reading a chapter of violence. Some human being had threshed out his life in agony on that sand; and Joe's sympathetic imagination reconstructed the scene detail by detail as the tracks suggested. Men had to die. Sure. But why, under the Western sky and with all the immense distances for freedom of use, did men have to ambush each other? Indigo's voice cut sharply across his pondering.

"Somebody on the porch."

They had traversed a gradual downward slope. A hundred yards to the fore stood a weathered, sagging frame shanty. Obviously a nester's home, for a fence with a single strand of wire boxed a few barren acres, and one small patch of ground had been scratched loose for a garden. A row of sunflowers skirted the house. A man sat motionless in a rocking chair near the front door.

The partners waited a moment for the customary invitation to light and rest. None came. Joe Breedlove stepped down, smiling cheerfully. "I reckon you'll pardon the intrusion. But it is a new country to us and we're wondering just what direction town is from here."

The man was very old and shriveled. His clothes hung loosely, showing the sharp points of his frame; the hands resting on the rocker arms were blackened by long years of sun and twisted by long years of work. And he had nothing to say to Joe in reply. At first it seemed to the genial partner that this old fellow was a mute, or deaf, or that age had drugged his tongue. He thought so only for a moment. The rocker stirred and began a slow swinging. The fellow's head came up and Joe saw misery in his faded blue eyes. Joe had seen torture of spirit before. He knew the stamp of it; he recognized it here. The old man swayed as if to soothe and relieve pain. Then the partners heard a strangled laboring of breath inside the house; such a weird and blood-chilling suspiration that Indigo tipped on his heels and threw a startled glance at his companion. Joe circled the rocker and entered the half darkened shanty.

There was a woman huddled in a dim corner; crying dismally. She had an apron thrown over her head and her hands were spread against the wall, slowly slipping to the floor. Joe started to back away, and stopped. Nearer the door and directly under a window was a bunk, occupied now with the rigid and lifeless body of a young puncher. A single blue spot stood out in startling clearness upon the gray and settled face.

"Nesters," whispered Indigo. "The kid was the support of the family. So some outfit plugged him to keep his kind out of the land. Damn 'em, Joe!"

"I reckon it's the end of the story, all right," agreed Joe, soberly. He went outside, staring into the distance. The serenity and the kindliness was gone from Joe then. "Somebody," said he, "ought to be crucified for that, Indigo, somebody ought to suffer!"

"Don't worry none, somebody will."

Both of them turned as if pulled by the same spring to face a newcomer slouched by the corner of the house. Where he had been the meanwhile or where he had come from they didn't know. But here he stood, a slim tall man with iron-gray hair and delicate fingers and a face that seemed as cold as marble. He was dressed like a circuit rider—string tie and white shirt and a black broadcloth suit. But there was no religion on the gentleman's face. He had been nurtured on a different training. Joe saw it instantly. Along the silver-haired partner's trail there had been other men like this—solitary and secretive and coldly watchful. He studied the man with an interest that seemed to intensify with each passing moment.

Indigo shifted, growing restive and angry under the newcomer's steady stare. "Glad to hear it. But what's the idea of slinking around the premises like a feline? I would also like to ask you if they's anything funny about my nose which makes you goggle at it so unmannerly?"

"Where are you strangers from?" inquired the man, bluntly.

"North," replied Joe.

"If it's any of your doggone' business," added Indigo with an equal bluntness.

"Where to?" snapped the inquisitor.

"South," drawled Joe. His blue eyes bored into the fellow's face. He smiled and Indigo, seeing the quality of that smile, stepped promptly aside and held his peace. "I reckon you'd be the gentleman called Dead Card John," pursued Joe in the same sleepy manner. "Your repute goes ahead to greet all pilgrims. A friend or relation of yours—the boy in there?"

All he had for an answer was a slight inclination of Dead Card John's head. Joe likewise nodded. "Yeah. And you'll maybe be writing somebody's ticket. I'd like to ask the caliber and make of your rifle, mister. Just to satisfy a curiosity."

"I give you credit," said Dead Card John, lids rising from his strange and unfathomable eyes. A man only got that kind of fixed expression through years at one particular vocation. As well as the cold and marble pallor of cheeks that defied sun and wind. "I give you credit," repeated Dead Card John, each word the more chilly. "But I won't answer that question. If you are riding south don't let me keep you waiting. And you might tell anybody who asks you in Terese," each syllable piling up to a higher, more biting and bitter pitch, "that Dead Card John's riding. You'll do me a favor."

Joe nodded. "Maybe I'll do it, if anybody asks me. But I reckon the country may know it before we get to Terese. I'm some accustomed to the West, friend. And which way is Terese, anyhow?"

"South along the valley," said Dead Card John. As the partners swung up and turned from the house he added another impersonally polite warning. "When you get there, I wouldn't be in any hurry to declare yourselves."

" 'Most every county has two kinds of politics," observed Joe. He spent a last penetrating look upon Dead Card John. "I reckon, friend, I've covered some little territory in the last sixteen years. It's been a long while since I was a younker setting out to see the world in '95. A fellow absorbs a heap. We bid you good day."

They passed a horse saddled and waiting. Joe gave it a quick inspection and passed on. The rifle boot was on the far side and he couldn't make out the fellow's weapon. Indigo grumbled for a half mile before arriving at a conviction.

"It might've been his bullet, Joe. What was he snooping around for? He sure registers poison to me. I've seen poker faces like his before."

"When we rounded the corner," mused Joe, "he'd put his hand on the old gent's shoulder."

Indigo looked queerly at his partner. "Say, for the love of Jupiter, Joe, are you a-trying to make out a case for that stone-eyed gent? It ain't like you. It ain't. Usually you're a man to ketch a fellow's disposition pretty quick. You'd ought to know he was poison."

"Well, to tell the truth," confessed Joe, almost meekly, "I found points about him I liked. Yeah, I did."

"All you're trying to do now is start an argument. You don't mean it. But what was the idee of throwing dates at him like you did. It ain't your habit to brag, Joe."

"Sometimes I naturally spill over with past history," murmured Joe. The blandness left him. "It ain't so much the dead youngster, Indigo. Well, it's hard enough for them kind to go. But it's the old ones. It gets me. I won't sleep well for some nights. Why has that got to be? Whenever I hear a woman cry like that—or an old man with a dead look in his eyes—it gets me, Indigo."

"Well, it ain't settled yet," grunted Indigo. "I sort of feel like we'll be in this deal." He looked at Joe from the corner of his eye, assaying the result of the remark. And when Joe nodded assent Indigo straightened and snorted like an impatient war horse. "Sometimes I understand you, Joe. Sometimes I do. This day sure is fading fast."

They cut down a sharp wall in the graying late afternoon and struck a winding road southward. A forty-foot river ran beside the road, and chrome bluffs narrowed and widened as they traveled. They accelerated pace, feeling the end of a long journey. The bluffs narrowed again and the road and river squeezed through nothing more than a slit of earth. Just beyond, the valley unfolded into a gray plain. Just beyond, also, was a roadside saloon with a light glimmering prematurely out of a smudged window. An isolated and lonely place meant for an isolated and lonely rendezvous. The partners, courting the same unspoken thought, reined before it, got down and stepped inside.

They faced a crowd. They interrupted a flow of heated talk. And as they came somewhat beyond the door one of that crowd turned with a clearly defensive movement and gave them a sharp and insolent glance out of his cynically humorous face. Cattle country was filled with such faces, but Joe marked it as he marched toward the bar. There was a flurry of laugh and a murmur. "Don't get excited none, Al. You're a long ways from Ox Bow country."

"Yeah," grinned the one who had turned so quickly. "I guess. Yeah."

Silence fell, a heavy, ill-humored silence that smothered the partners like so much foul air. Indigo's hackles instantly rose, but Joe turned to him with a mild glance and spoke soothingly to a sullen barkeep.

"A little rye, Doctor."

The barkeep passed a glance toward the crowd and seemed to find an answer. "Ain't got no rye, friend."

Joe smiled. "Kentucky's best, then."

The barkeep turned his seal-fat back to them and ran a heavy eye along shelves plentifully laden. He scanned the rows of bottles and swung. "I don't reckon we got anything you'd care to drink," he decided with some emphasis.

Indigo's washed-out orbs took on a glitter that meant but

one thing. Joe checked him again, still smiling. He reached into his pocket and extracted therefrom a gold five-dollar piece. He laid it very carefully in front of the barkeep and took a pace backward, drawing his gun with a deliberateness that was outrageously indecent. And he scanned the bottles on the shelves until he found a label that attracted his eye. The gun rose, a single explosion filled the room and shook the loose window sashes. The bottle fell apart, throwing its amber liquid to the floor in successive spurts.

"A little American, then," murmured Joe, holstering the gun. "Obliged for the hospitality. Come on, Indigo."

They went out and rode through the deepening haze. Indigo poured a hot stream of invective into the damp air. Presently the lights of Terese town enfolded them. They stabled their horses and turned toward the saloon for that drink which preceded a well-balanced meal.

"I'll live to pull that roadside dump into the crick," fumed Indigo, breaking out afresh. "I'll see it lying in charred ashes. You'd think we was greasers the way our money don't talk."

"Wasn't that," murmured Joe, pushing against the saloon's swinging door. "That gang was up to something. We walked into a private meeting. That dead boy is only a chapter, Indigo. It ain't the whole story—only a chapter."

The saloon was a glittering and gaudy Western palace. It was a three-ringed circus where a man might at the same time drink, gamble and be entertained. A bar ran the full length of the place, a stage jutted out from the far end and there was no limit save the sky on the amount of money to be played across the rows of tables. A sign above the bar said as much. Around the ornate paneling were the fighters of three generations and the dancing girls and soubrettes beloved of the land; a goldfish paddled wearily around an immense glass bowl, a piano chattered *Dixie* in different keys. And a gentleman of ample proportions and expensive broadcloth clothing raised a hand to the partners as they slouched to the bar.

"Strangers here?"

"No formal introductions yet," gravely acquiesced Joe.

The gentleman crooked his finger at a near barkeep. "First drink is always on my house. I serve good drinks, boys. I keep the crowd entertained. And I don't talk politics much. From which direction did you sift in? The question ain't meant personal."

"We met a fellow called Dead Card John," murmured Joe and raised a ruby glass. His blue eyes met those of the saloonkeeper blandly. Yet by that one glance he made known to the saloonkeeper the kind of man he was. Through the years Joe Breedlove established friends on that short a notice. The saloonkeeper rolled his cigar and crooked another finger. He poured himself a drink and lifted it ceremoniously. "I will wet the occasion with you. The person with the blue chin and red pug face over yonder is Crowheart Ames."

Joe eased himself around and passed a mild, incurious glance through the room. His attention fell aimlessly on the designated citizen, lingered inconspicuously and returned to the saloon proprietor. "Does he own this town or did nature put that look on his geography?"

"Sheriff of Terese County, friend," said the saloon man softly. "I don't talk politics much."

"I'm so hungry," sighed Indigo, "that I feel like a post hole which ain't been filled up. Le's eat."

"Yeah," drawled Joe, not at all following the import of his partner's words. "There's a table over by the sheriff gent. We sit there a minute, Indigo. Just to rest and ponder."

They rolled casually through the crowd and sat down. Joe relaxed like a man very tired, and his eyes seemed to be closed. But Indigo knew better and he fidgeted in the chair and composed himself to follow Joe's game, not knowing what it was, or why it should concern Crowheart Ames. Joe's left eyelid fluttered and rose to command the sheriff's table. The sheriff was not alone. A dancing girl sat opposite him, dressed in a hoop skirt. That skirt and the tune of *Dixie* being thumped out on the piano indicated the variety of play that was about to be brought forth upon the stage. But the girl, Joe decided, was not Southern. She had yellow hair and her eyes were gray in the lamplight. She was young, she touched a glass before her with a gesture of refusal, and she seemed uncomfortable in the company of Crowheart Ames.

Crowheart looked to be a politician nurtured on whisky. The man's face dished like that of an English bull; it was broad and pudgy and somewhat red. He slouched in his chair, with a puckered grin on his cheeks. Joe didn't care much for the grin and from what his eyes gathered, neither did the girl. Indigo kicked his foot under the table and looked significantly toward the door. Joe turned to see two newcomers enter the saloon. One was a stunted and sheepish puncher better than half drunk. The other man Joe instantly recognized. It was Al, he of the cynically humorous face, who had so quickly turned to inspect the partners at the roadside joint.

The sight of these two affected the crowd in the saloon queerly. The droning of talk rose to a higher note as man after man turned to look at the pair. Joe's shrewd eyes skipped from table to table, marking the nodding heads and the sudden twisting of lips in whispered speech. Through the rumbling and through the heavy smoke floated a name —"Praygood Nuggins." It reached Joe. It reached the sheriff, whose fat jowls settled. He had been talking to the girl but he broke off instantly and twisted in his chair, scowling.

The man whose name Joe knew to be Al, swung toward the bar, refusing to look at the sheriff, but the half-drunken puncher seemed to catch hold of Crowheart Ames's pug face as a familiar and friendly beacon. He made for the sheriff, marvelously navigating the twisting lane between tables. And he fumbled in a bulging pocket and caught something in his horny hands. Crowheart Ames shook his head. "Get away from here, Snipe. You're drunk, disgusting drunk. Get away from here before I lock you up."

Snipe's fist fell to the sheriff's table and opened. A pair of bullet slugs rolled along the surface; Snipe grinned and waggled his finger. "Fooled you that time, Mister Ames. I'm on 'ficial business. Tha's your invite to Rube Mamerock's fandango tomorrow night. Don' forget to bring them invites or you'll be turned back cold at the bridge. Them invites is marked. They is also sleepered and no son-of-a-gun can forge an invite. You may be sheriff, Mister Ames, but Rube Mamerock's fandango starts at dark tomorrow. You be there. Throw me in jail? Not when I'm on Rube Mamerock's 'ficial business. You'd sure regret it, Mister Ames."

He turned away with a grand and final gesture of his twisted arm and started back. His attention centered upon the partners and he stopped immediately and stared at them long and profoundly. "Lessee—don't guess I give you an invite." Down into his pocket he went. Two more leaden slugs rolled across the table top and were caught by Joe's flat palm. "Invite to Rube Mamerock's fandango. Tomorrow night. Don't forget them invites. Got to have 'em to cross the bridge. You be there."

"Thanks," said Joe. He studied the slugs carefully. Upon the rounding top of each was a rough cross. And around the body of each was a deep furrow. He raised his mild eyes to the puncher. "What outfit is this, friend, and where's it at?"

The question seemed both to sober and insult the messenger. He made a move as if to retrieve the slugs and failed because Joe Breedlove's palm closed securely over them. He straightened and spoke with a tremendous dignity.

"I nev' thought a soul in this county didn't know Rube Mamerock's Ox Bow outfit. When you die, mister, and step inside the gate of paradise you'll see some fine range. But it won't compete with Ox Bow. Ox Bow Ranch is half of Terese County, stranger. And the other half ain't worth bothering about. When it's roundup time on Ox Bow the state stops to listen to the rumble of hoofs. When Ox Bow ships, they's a solid string of cars from here to Omaha. Ox Bow leather is on your boots and Ox Bow beef has foddered you since you was a child, no matter was you raised in Arizona or Montana. I'm an Ox Bow rider and though I may be drunk I will rise to state calmly I'd ruther peel spuds on said ranch than own the brand of any other peanut outfit in Terese. Texas is a big state, Ox Bow is bigger. Rube Mamerock made it thataway and when—" he paused and turned a complete circle, feeling the focus of a hundred eyes and the complete silence of the room—"and when the time comes for old Rube to hang up his saddle and lay away his rope; when said time comes hell will sure be a mild climate compared to Terese County!"

Crowheart Ames roared savagely. "Get out of here, you soak!" The dancing girl's face whitened and she leaned across the table, speaking softly. Crowheart's sudden, blunt speech cut from corner to corner of the place.

"Why hold it back any longer? Everybody knows but you, Ray. Girl, Sam Trago was shot to ribbons out by his daddy's shanty this morning. He's stone dead, kid."

A scream slashed the heavy air and tore like a knife through Joe Breedlove's heart. To a man the crowd rose up, chairs squealing across the floor. And speech roared from wall to wall, heavy and profane. The dancing girl had fainted, her yellow head lying on the table top. Crowheart rose and circled beside her.

The saloon proprietor plunged against the milling bodies, spitting ire at the sheriff. "Keep your paws off her. Did you have to bust it on the girl like that? You damn' fool!"

Crowheart had the girl in his arms. And then, from a different angle of this room, Joe noticed the slim figure of Dead Card John threading forward. He had not been in the place until now, that much was certain. Nor had he entered by the front way. But here he was in front of Crowheart Ames, marble cheeks cut with deep lines, eyes burning incredibly bright. He extended his arms and Crowheart, saying no word and making no protest, surrendered the girl. Joe Breedlove sighed when he saw how Dead Card John looked down upon the dancing girl's yellow hair. "By God, Indigo, I like that man!" A lane opened and closed. Dead Card John disappeared with his burden.

"Who's Sam Trago?" asked Indigo.

"The boy we saw dead."

"Yeah, I know that. I guessed it. But I wonder who he was."

"Just a chapter, Indigo. Just a chapter, not the whole story. Have you observed how quick this dude Al and also Dead Card John reached town behind us?"

Both partners were diverted. Once more the name of a man swept through the place, the name of Praygood Nuggins. The saloon entrance was blocked by a figure; and Joe, whose whole training had made him sensitive to mob sentiment, knew then and there that Terese was afraid of the newcomer. A tremendous struggle unfolded while the raw and uncertain night closed down.

CHAPTER 2

Fifty-one years, lacking a day—the anniversary was more religiously remembered and celebrated on Ox Bow than the Fourth of July—Rube Mamerock had ridden his jaded horse to the edge of a bluff and looked down upon a river and a flat and fair land rolling away beyond the river. Rube Mamerock had been very young then. Very young and poor. Fever was in his native Texas, the fever that racked men's bones; Rube, stopping to rove the far reaches of this new country with his hungry eyes, was a gaunt and malarial scarecrow seeking for a home.

The War of Sections was just over and in the deep Southwest it was being rumored that railroads were building across to Kansas and that cattle could be driven northward, to be fattened and shipped. Rube had left Texas with the rumor in his ears and he had traveled until he witnessed with his own eyes the twin steel rails creeping across the Kansas prairie. And so, seeing the virgin lands marching beyond the river, he got down from his horse, squatted in the sand and traced his initials.

"I reckon I'll stick here till the Indians drive me out."

He was the first cattleman in the region. He antedated the state government. He himself had named Terese County and town after the single drab woman ever to cross the undeviating path of his career. And she had tarried but a moment, for Rube Mamerock had starved so long as a youth that all his adult years were marked by an incessant hunger after material possessions. He wanted nothing else, worked for nothing else. Now, with a full seventy years upon his shoulders, he sat on the veranda of his house and looked out upon the same scene he had discovered so long ago. And all that he saw was his property. Land and cattle and barns and corrals. No other ranch in Terese was an eighth as large. He had arrived first, taken the best and the most; and the result was a virtual kingdom at once the wonder and the envy of the surrounding country.

Rube Mamerock made it; and it, in turn, left a mark on Rube. All the labor and the fighting and the riding showed on this old man. At seventy he was done. In fact he had been coasting for several years; watching the distances from his porch—a heavy, white-haired gentleman with incredibly deep lines upon his face and with muscles half useless. When he tamped down his pipe, the fingers of his hands trembled with a palsy. He had created a small empire, his job was done. Yet, in all the breadth of the land, Rube Mamerock knew of no kin, no relation of any degree to whom he could surrender his achievement. There was none of his own blood to keep the Ox Bow going.

A stunted, diffident puncher rolled awkwardly up from the corrals. "That claybank hoss ain't no good in ary manner, shape nor form, boss. Might just as well turn it back to the wild bunch."

Rube Mamerock ducked his white head. "All right. And when you go by the sheds, Snipe, send Sam Trago up here."

Snipe looked at his boss questioningly. "Why, Sam he went over to his folks' place this morning."

Mamerock frowned at his pipe. "Sure. Why didn't I remember that? Sent him off myself." He pushed his unsteady frame out of the chair and limped to the steps with the gait of one whose bones were brittle. "I'm getting some old, Snipe. Even my mind's falling back on me." He propped himself by a post and watched the distant hills wistfully. "Rain over there. Going to be a wet winter, Snipe. I always said I wanted to be buried in warm ground. It'll be damp, Snipe, damn' damp, when you boys put me away."

Snipe twisted, uncomfortable. "Shucks, that's no kind of palaver for Rube Mamerock. You're good for a lot of wear yet. Say, what would become of Ox Bow—?"

Mamerock's black eyes turned thoughtfully on the diminutive Snipe. "My boy, I figured that question five years before I found an answer."

Snipe muttered an astonished, "Son-of-a-gun! Didn't know you had any heirs."

"None," growled Mamerock. "Now shut up. I'll be announcing all details to Terese County tomorrow night. Get busy, Snipe. How's she stand now?"

"Barbecue pits is dug. Ten three-year-old steers in the pen. We slaughters and dresses 'em first off in the morning. We got twenty gallons of rye and thirty of Kentucky corn liquor coming out late today. Doctor is hollering his head off about the cooking he's got to do but there's a heap of provisions he's turned out. Nothing short I can figure."

"Invitations?"

"Done," said Snipe and turned up the palms of his hands. "Yeah, that labor is likewise finished."

"Put them in the usual sacks, Snipe. Hitch the buckboard. I'm sending you around to distribute them this year. Sam Trago's going to be too busy. Come back here when you're ready to go."

Snipe went off at a gait between a limp and a run. Rube Mamerock filled his pipe and walked away from his house toward the rear. Fifty years gone he had built his first log hut at the same spot, facing the bluffs; for at that time the river ran directly below the high chrome walls. Later, in his flush years, Rube Mamerock had carted stone seventy miles from the railroad to build the tremendous and lonely pile of masonry he now tenanted. And the porch was moved around to face the other way. The river no longer crept by the foot of the bluffs. It had gouged another channel. Across that channel was a long wooden bridge, battered by the years of usage, connecting Mamerock home quarters with his range and the outside world. The bluff hemmed him in at the rear; and though the old channel was dry, there were occasional wet winters in which water coursed through it. At such times the Ox Bow home ranch was on an island. The porous sands of that ancient course were damp this afternoon with the seepage of a rising main channel. Mamerock watched the ragged clouds up in the peaks.

"First time in seven seasons I've had wet weather for the fandango." He tried to light his match and was balked by his unsteady fingers. Once, such a physical defect would have put him in a towering rage. Today he shoved the pipe in his pocket and raised his white head to the horizons. "Rube, old man, what are you kicking about? Ain't it been a great life? I remember when I carved my initials in the sand up on the bluff top. Hell of a long while ago. Said I'd stay till the Indians drove me out. Indians all gone. Pretty soon old Rube'll be gone. Well, when a man starts looking at the trail behind him it's high time he did go. Only I had to wait till Sam Trago grew up and got hardened in." Habit caused him to reach for his pipe again. This time he got it lit. "Sam'll take care of the buzzards. By St. Mary's bells they been waiting a long time for me to die! Sam'll fool 'em."

Snipe drove across the yard with the buckboard and stopped. "Any orders?"

Mamerock shook his head. "You know the folks I always ask to come. Find 'em and leave an invite. Don't get drunk. And don't pass out any invite to the buzzards. Remember that, Snipe. It's been a pride of mine to honor every invite presented at the bridge. They're the same as old Rube Mamerock's word, no matter whose fists they get into. The buzzards know that, Snipe. So see you don't give any the wrong way. And don't get drunk. Hustle on. And say—" His cheeks fell away from the accustomed hardness; he almost smiled. "You might stop in at the saloon or the hotel and find Ray Chasteen. Say to her I'm counting time till I hear her sing tomorra."

"Leave a invite to her?" questioned Snipe.

"No, you fool brute!" snapped Mamerock. "What's the need one for? She's Sam Trago's girl, ain't she? He'll bring her. Go on, drag a line."

Snipe tooled the buckboard down the drive and across the insecure bridge. The old baron of Terese watched the puncher go eastward. And when the vehicle was but a dim blur in the distance he turned about and walked to the house. "The buzzards will sure be disappointed when I announce tomorrow that Sam Trago inherits the Ox Bow, lock, stock and barrel. They been waiting to pick up the pieces. God condemn 'em, they ain't powerful enough to hurt old Rube Mamerock when he's alive and they won't dare touch Sam Trago when I'm gone! I'd been dead long ago if I didn't know I had to hang on till Sam got hardened to man's work. Now I can die."

He got to the porch and sat down, letting his eyes roam away into the southern distances he knew and loved so well. Over a half century Rube Mamerock had watched the horizon in all its rounding moods. It was as much a part of him as his right hand. "Heaven," he murmured, "may be a fair country, but I'll sort of miss this." He struggled with his pipe and looked at his trembling fingers with mild disapproval. "Just falling to pieces. Worse the last three weeks. A heap worse. Well, one more chore done and I'll sleep well. I want Sam should wed Ray Chasteen in my place right sudden now. Nothing to keep me going then. Rube, you been a tough one. I'm sort of proud of what you did. Anxious to see what Gabriel's got tallied ag'in me on the book. Sam and Ray—they'll do well. Yeah, right well. The buzzards will sure go hungry."

So he pondered, smoking his pipe, feeling the cold tide of dissolution creep inexorably along his body, knowing that for him the race was all but run and that in just a little while all there would be of Rube Mamerock was a scar on the earth and a pine board with his name and a single date.

Snipe drove briskly east in the direction of Terese town, gloomy and cheerful by turns. Snipe was a simple soul and worshiped his outfit and his boss with a single-tracked devotion. So he was cast down when he thought of the boss passing away, and he whistled the *Cowboy's Lament* until he remembered he hadn't had a drink for going on two months and he hadn't cuked roulette for even longer than that.

"Gosh, but I'm scandalous thirsty. I'll go get me a drink. Just one little drink. Then I'll spurn the redeye and be on my way. What was that system I doped out for bucking roulette, anyhow? Sure was a hummer. Got to remember that."

He held the reins between his knees and with a stub of a pencil and a fragment of wrapping paper, plunged into an intricate system of gambling. The team put the miles behind, the land rose and fell with its endless sweeping billows. They passed a shanty, they galloped over a bridge. A horseman, unseen by the preoccupied Snipe, raced parallel on a remote bridge and drew gradually inward, arriving at the road some little distance ahead of Snipe. As the rig passed, the horseman had a clear look of the canvas bags and since he was an old hand in the country, he knew what Snipe's mission was. He galloped in pursuit.

"Hey there, Snipe!"

Snipe bobbed in the seat and looked around with a half guilty air. The horseman waved a hand. "Pull down, kid, pull down. What's the idea of snubbing a friend thataway?"

"Oh, hello there, Al," muttered Snipe weakly. He stopped the rig. "Say, I wasn't snubbing nobody. Jus' a-doing some personal bookkeeping. Yeah."

Al grinned; and that grin made his slack and cynical face even more unlovely. He had a mouth the size and shape of an Indian's and it sat unbalanced between a hatchet chin and a grotesque Roman nose. Snipe shifted his weight uneasily under Al's long and knowing stare. "Listen, Al," he protested, "you're allus making fun of me. Cut it out. Ain't I got a right to bookkeep?"

"Where you going, Snipe?"

"Town," mumbled Snipe and fiddled with the reins. He wanted to be on his way, but he was too mild a soul to achieve bluntness with a man like Al.

Al looked at the canvas bags and winked. "Peddling invites to old Rube's party, uh?"

"Yeah," said Snipe and stared absently at his feet.

"Well, that's sure fine. I never did have drag enough to get an invite from him yet. But seeing you're a friend of mine, why gimme one, Snipe."

Snipe colored a little. "Now look here, Al, you and me is friends. I know we used to ride together. But I got strict orders about these invites. It ain't my place to pass 'em promiscuous. I don't believe I better do it."

"So I ain't good enough for you, huh?" snorted Al, manufacturing a presentable show of anger. "I never figured a friend would ever toss me like that."

"Aw, hell, Al, you know better," protested Snipe, feeling pretty miserable. "Ain't I said I got orders?"

"What's the matter with me?" demanded Al.

Snipe fidgeted. Diplomacy was no part of his training, yet he had need of careful words here. "Well, I ain't got the slightest doubt of your character, Al. Say, I'd lend you ten bucks—if I had ten bucks. I ain't forgetting we got drunk many a time, side by side. But you're trailing with Praygood Nuggins. My old man sure has got a canker against Praygood. You know it same's me. Well, how would it look if I give you an invite? Nossir, I don't dast."

"Nuggins," was Al's severe retort, "is a man of integrity."

"Sure, sure," Snipe hastened to state. "I ain't casting no aspersions on his character, am I?" Privately, Snipe thought Nuggins to be a thorough scoundrel, but he skipped and slid nimbly around his inner convictions. He was afraid of rousing Al's wrath. He stood in fear of Al, as a matter of fact. In other days, this grinning chap always had managed to bully or cajole or trick Snipe into meek obedience. Snipe was no warrior, when sober.

"Well, I'm sure glad to hear you ain't," Al muttered, with an ominous note. "Going to town? Yeah, well move over and I'll ride on the seat with you and lead my hoss."

Snipe disliked this but he gave room and clucked his tongue. The team went on. Al made a gesture toward his pocket and brought out a flask. "Have a drink, Snipe."

Snipe gave birth to a feeble groan. "Al, I oughtn't do it. Honest. You know me. Either I keep off it total or else I get so drunk I'm filthy. And considering what I got to do yet—"

Al raked him with a shrewd sidewise glance and appeared tremendously outraged. "Listen, Snipe, you wasn't too good for me once. I take that personal. I sure take it personal. By gravy, I got a good notion to resent it!"

"Well, Al," mumbled Snipe, "you got me wrong complete. And just to show you I'm the same big-hearted fella I allus was I'll take a nip. Gimme the bottle."

"Fine. I knowed you was a friend. Let it trickle down."

Snipe seized the bottle, tipped it to the gray afternoon's sky and made a bow. He drank and looked around to Al, a different man. There was a quality in corn liquor that had the power of transforming Snipe almost instantly. At heart, this small and meek puncher felt unequal with the world. His very stature, contrasted with those robust riders continually around him, put a handicap on his pride. But once he resorted to the bottle all barriers of size, distance and time fell. Snipe, when sober, had his dreams of making a lion of himself. When drunk this remote and well-buried ambition flamed up like a crusading torch. His voice changed, his glance became more severe, he spoke more gruffly.

"Listen, Al, is this the only bottle you got?"

"Yeah."

"That's too bad," stated Snipe. "It sure is too bad. I aim to drink it here and now."

"Save a mite for me," protested Al, though the protest was half-hearted.

"I'll save the bottle, that's all. Here's mud in your eyes." Half of that flask's contents vanished. Snipe's cheeks took on color. His eyes glittered; he tipped his small chin upward and gave Al a hard, hard look. "Al, move over in this seat. I don't like to be crowded."

"You and me used to be friends," mourned Al, giving room.

"We still is," declared Snipe crisply. "But as for that sheep-stealing, wolf-hearted, stone-eyed Praygood Nuggins you is chumming with—I wouldn't touch him with a ten-foot pole. He's the biggest skunk in Terese. He's skulking around Ox Bow like a yellow mongrel, waiting for old Rube to kick the beam. Well, he sure has got some astonishment coming to him."

Al's interest focused. "What's that?"

"Don't spit at me thataway or I'll kick you off this vehicle."

"All right, don't get sore. But what's on Rube's chest?"

"None of your business. You'll discover in proper time. Al, I ain't going to tell you but once more to move over in this seat and gimme room."

"Hell!" exploded Al, "I'm sitting clear off in space now! Well, I never figured a day like this to come. You and me was friends once."

"We still is," asserted Snipe irately. He leaned back and ripped open the top of a canvas bag. Quite impressively he brought forth a single leaden slug. "I tell you—I'm going to give you this invite. It's an act of pure kindness on my part which you ain't sensible enough to appreciate. Some-

78

times I like you—sometimes I don't. Your good instincks is good—but your bad instincks is manifold and plumb putrid."

Al accepted the slug with patent eagerness. He grinned broadly at Snipe and relaxed. "I won't ever tell who give it to me."

"That's right—keep it dark." Snipe drained the remaining half of the bottle and threw it into the sagebrush with great violence. There had been only a pint in it to begin with, but Snipe's last drink had been a month previous and moreover he was of that unfortunate breed to whom a swallow was as deadly as a gallon. He clutched the reins and shouted a shrill "Eeeeyip!" He threw his hat after the now distant bottle and swayed in the rocketing buggy. He seized the brake handle and seemed about to tear it away from the vehicle. "Say, what makes us go so doggone' slow? Al, quit dragging your feet on the ground or I'll kick you off the stage!"

"You're going faster'n the law allows right now," said Al. "Better slow down a little."

Snipe stood up, thus imperiling his life; he lashed the rumps of the horses with the rein ends and cried weirdly into the deepening dusk of the afternoon. Al pulled him into the seat, at which Snipe launched into a long and detailed account of Al's ancestors. All of whom turned out to be extraordinarily depraved in the narrative. Al bided his time, seeming to weigh the quality of Snipe's drunkenness. Now and again he stole a look at the open bags of slugs within easy arm's reach and once he dropped a casual fist in that direction. But Snipe saw the move and challenged his friend with unmistakable sharpness. "Cut that out!" Al desisted, knowing from experience just how far it was safe to trespass with an inebriated Snipe. Presently he tried another tack.

"Say, Snipe, ain't you going to give me an invite?"

Snipe gravely debated this. "Didn't I give you one just now?"

"Nope. You only said you was going to give me one. I ain't got it yet. You're drunk."

"I ain't drunk." He fell into a profound study, emerging with this definite conviction. "About that invite—I figure I give you an invite. If I did give you one, that's all right, though I oughtn't to have done it. But if I didn't give you an invite, that's all right, too, because you ain't got one coming. Both ways don't make no difference. I ain't going to do neither. Is that Terese up in the distance? Sure enough. Pile out and ride your hoss into town. I got a reppitation to maintain and I don't allow no Nuggins hirelings to be seen with me."

79

Al departed from the vehicle, mounted his pony and galloped headlong into the prairie, skirting Terese and continuing toward the high and colorful ramparts some two miles or more ahead. Snipe entered Terese with the team at a dead run. He stabled his team, filled his pockets with the unique invitations, hid the rest in the hay, and sallied forth to do his chore. He did it with commendable exactness, too, for an hour or better. But around dusk an unquenched thirst drew him to the saloon. Al appeared out of the shadows and the two of them entered together. The hot air made Snipe's head very woolly and from that moment onward he lost his bearings. He marked the sheriff with a glad heart. He saw the partners and gave to each a slug, thinking them to be somebody else. He delivered his oration and proceeded to the bar, glowing with pride of achievement. Thenceforth he was a lost soul and the buzzards—lying in wait—began to close in. Al kept at a discreet distance, supplying Snipe with whisky.

CHAPTER 3

Praygood Nuggins stood inside the saloon only a moment; but in that moment Joe Breedlove knew that he had accomplished some definite purpose, sent out a clear warning to somebody. He turned toward the full light of the room and Joe, eyes half closed, caught an unforgettable picture. Nuggins had the body of a veteran cavalryman; he carried himself like one. A silver-yellow mustache guarded a thin and grimly-set mouth—the mouth of a man who first had conquered himself before setting out upon a hard career. Above the mustache was a thin and swooping nose. His cheekbones were high, on a line with a pair of almond-shaped eyes that, catching the lights of the room, threw back an immensely cold gleam. Joe, who loved to draw figures out of the past and compare them with present actors, found no face in the long gallery of his memory to match that of Praygood Nuggins. It was flinty and dominant and with no single spark of compassion upon it. A hush fell across the saloon. Indigo, instinctively hostile on sight of such a man, muttered a sour phrase. Praygood Nuggins made a precise half-circle on his heels and was gone. It was as if a heavy hand had been lifted from the crowd. Voices rose.

"Let's go," grumbled Indigo. "How many times have I got to tell you I'm slowly passing away with hunger. I got to have nutriment. Joe, they is something almighty big smoking up hereabouts and somehow I don't feel equal to the occasion. I feel sort of like a two-bit ante in a thousand-dollar pot."

"You spoke words of wisdom," murmured Joe, filing away in his mind the fact that the cynical-cheeked Al was making his exit with a leisured and apparently aimless manner. The partners sauntered toward the door. Joe pulled toward the counter and signaled for another drink. It was not entirely accidental that he slid into a space beside the saloon proprietor.

That gentleman dropped his head a scant half inch in recognition of the maneuver. "The gent was Praygood Nuggins. I don't talk politics much."

"I reckon we've seen pro and con hereabouts in the last ten minutes," drawled Joe.

"A fact," assented the saloon man. He studied Joe with a closer interest. "I could stand to see more of you, friend. Drop in for a quiet drink some morning."

"Who was Sam Trago?" asked Joe, hoisting his glass.

"Rube Mamerock's right-hand man," grunted the saloon proprietor. "That's the Ox Bow, for which I note you received an invite. Figure to be some present tomorrow night?"

"Yeah."

The saloon man shrugged his ample shoulders. "I'm going also. It's the fifty-first year of Rube's rule in these parts. And —" with a gentle slurring of the words—"his last."

Joe drank and turned the glass between his fingers. "A tough old duck, huh?"

"A square old duck," added the saloonkeeper with emphasis. He frowned and looked around him. "It's been said, friend, that Rube ain't got no heirs. I have also heard it passed he might pass the outfit on to Sam Trago." Then, as if he had gone beyond the limit of discretion, he covered the statement with a quick phrase. "You know how them things is speculated. Judge for yourself. You know cattle country."

"Yeah," drawled Joe and looked the saloon man directly in the face. "What might be that fine girl's name?"

"Ray Chasteen. She was to've married Sam Trago next week." The saloon man's anger swelled out of him. "Damn that clumsy Crowheart!"

"A pretty name," mused Joe, shoving the glass away from him. "I sure like your layout here, friend. Reminds me of Abilene a long time back. When I was a kid once in Abilene—" He nodded at the proprietor and moved away with Indigo.

The partners stepped into the deep night. It had begun to rain and the gentle patter sounded on the shingles and in the dirt soothingly. There was a fog sifting through Terese. Lights made round crystal sprays in the gloom. A restaurant's door was wide open across the street and the partners entered and slouched by the counter. Joe seemed drowsy.

"Who was Sam Trago?" grumbled Indigo, repeating the question for the third time in the last six hours. "Yeah, I know what we've picked up, but it don't make much sense to me."

"He's through," said Joe and waved his hand with a flip of finality. "But the rest of it ain't hardly started. We're in on this, Indigo."

"I see a sign ten-foot high which reads: Keep Out," countered Indigo, his unlovely face overladen with a dyspeptic pessimism. "You know me, Joe. I ain't usually a fellow to keep out of trouble. I wades in it some often. But this is sure swift water. It's over my head—and I ain't able to swim a lick."

A weary waitress dropped platters and cups before them, spilling coffee on the counter. And her only apology was a sharp demand for money. "Two bits each, in advance. We don't feed boomers free."

Both of Indigo's hands were busy with his provender. Joe slid a half-dollar toward the girl. His gray eyes touched the girl and he smiled, the rare and mellow sympathy and humor of the man crinkling in the sun-etched furrows around his temples. The girl lowered her chin. Twin spots of color spread over her cheeks. And she smiled back at him wanly. "I get tired sometimes, Whitey. Forget it. When you empty that coffee cup I'll bring more." She retreated to the kitchen.

Joe tackled his meat. "Nevertheless, it's our party, Indigo."

Indigo waggled his head in astonishment. "Sometimes you're a mystified puzzle to me. What was that remark about peace being your pet horse?"

Joe turned to his partner, all the bland pleasantry gone. A grim, tremendous anger blazed in its place. The transformation was so startling that even Indigo, who had before seen the destructive power of this tall and even-tempered man, was set back. "Indigo, it sticks in my throat! That old gent sitting on the shanty porch. That lady crying in the shadows with an apron over her head. By God, I'll kill somebody for that! It ain't right to strike folks like them so hard that they're cut clean to the bone. Sam Trago's dead. A bullet don't hurt when it drills straight. But the old folks is on the rack. It'll kill 'em by degrees. That's what gets me. Somebody's going to satisfy me for doing that!"

Indigo swashed the coffee around the rim of his cup and downed it. He had finished, and there was nothing but wreckage to mark the course of his swift and devastating hunger. Sated, he relaxed, rolled a cigarette and filled his chest with smoke. "Hope I never get that hollow again. I feel more like m'self. Well, if you feel thataway about it I'll play a hand. But when we ram into grief and have to run out hell-bent for election, I don't want no sassy remarks about my ungoverned temper. There's my insurance. Now which?"

"Better sleep on it, I guess," said Joe.

They went out. The rain had strengthened, pouring out of a dead-black sky in heavy sheets. The shimmering lights fell across a street half awash. Roofs boomed, thunder rolled in from the distance. All other sounds in Terese town were muted. Men ran clumsily for shelter. The partners hugged the building walls in their progress toward the hotel. A phrase of Spanish and a stale smell of whisky and tobacco lifted against their faces; Joe's arm extended to warn Indigo. They stopped in the thick shadow of a porch.

Ten feet onward a door opened into a dim-lit Mexican saloon and café. A familiar face crossed the threshold and was lost in the street. Directly afterward they heard Snipe feebly protesting. He, too, was nearing that entrance; boots ripped the insecure planking of the walk and then the partner saw his shrunken, swaying body pilloried in the doorway's yellow square. There was a man holding him upright but they couldn't see who Snipe struggled with.

"Hey, Al, cut it out. Lay loose your doggone' paws or I'll belt you. I ain't had a drink all night and you're—whup—keeping me from ser'ous business. Lemme go."

"Want you should meet a particular friend of mine," said Al, voice rising against the swashing echo of the rain. "Best friend I got, outside of you, Snipe. It's sort of hurt him he didn't get no invite."

"Who's it?" plaintively demanded Snipe. "Keep y' paws off me. Get away from my pockets. Tell you, I'll give your friend a invite. Keep your paws off me! Where's this dude?"

"Meet my friend. Give him an invite like a good fellow."

All the partners saw of this third man was a long arm that extended out of the dark, reached into the lighted area of the door and took Snipe's veering arm. After that Snipe was shut from view. A flurry of words went up to the sky. Thunder roared. Then Al and Snipe were coming toward the partners, arguing. Joe and Indigo flattened themselves against the building wall to let them pass on. They were swallowed up.

Joe's grip on Indigo's arm constricted. "There's friend Al's most particular friend. They argued that little play very well."

Praygood Nuggins's gaunt frame slid into the Mexican joint. The door closed.

"Why hold a meeting out in this wet?" grumbled Indigo. "Was the gent afraid to show his face to that warped little Snipe runt?"

"I reckon Nuggins wanted an invite pretty bad," observed Joe, "and couldn't get it any other way. Nuggins staged all this. Guess he's not popular around Ox Bow. Even so, what's the idea of practically stealing an invite when he ain't welcome on Rube Mamerock's premises? It ain't quite clear. Indigo, tuck this fellow Al's face in your vest pocket. Nuggins owns his shirt."

"Not in my vest pocket," muttered Indigo. "I got a forty-dollar watch I don't want stopped."

They left the shelter and plunged across the street to the hotel, signed for a room and went up the stairs and down a dismal hall. The room faced the street and was a cheerless cubicle with flimsy, unpainted walls. Water dripped from a spot in the ceiling, windows rattled. They lit the lamp and set it in a far corner where the passing spurts of air disturbed it least. Indigo sprawled on the bed while Joe settled in a chair, rocking it back and forth to assemble and digest the strange, mysterious things he had seen and heard this long afternoon. Indigo closed his green orbs and addressed the ceiling.

"I figure this much. Rube Mamerock's got a nice lush outfit. He's about to blow out the candle and ascend to them sweet realms where they's music and rest. He ain't got no heirs. It's hinted his riding boss, Sam Trago, is the lucky man. But they's orders in the county which hone to steal, control or assume said ranch. So, Sam Trago dies. Am I right?"

"Yeah," drawled Joe. "Now proceed to the interesting part."

Indigo threw up his hands and rolled face down on the bed. "Hell, it's got me exhausted to get that far. The rest is all gummed in mystery. Mystery's your dish, not mine. You do the guessing. Tell me how these gents fit in."

Joe swayed in the rocker, staring through the wet panes. "Nuggins," said he, drowsily, "is a proud man. That girl loved Sam Trago, which is certain. They say Rube Mamerock's word ruled Terese. If he owns more'n half of the real estate in it, why shouldn't he have the say-so? Well, wolves always travel after a steer in packs. In packs, not single, Indigo. And a prize like this Ox Heart is sure to draw the greedy and the overweening. Crowheart Ames—now there's a man I wouldn't trust. I don't like that whisky smile. Did you observe how narrow his eyes were set, Indigo? As for Dead Card John, it looked this afternoon like there was plenty of riders in Terese scared of him. I wouldn't be surprised none. Two gents the county's scared of—" He bent forward, nose against the window pane. "Two that we know about—Dead Card John and this Praygood Nuggins." His body went out of the rocker as if shot by a catapult, his big brown hand whipped across the lamp globe's top and plunged the room in darkness. Indigo reared from the bed to find his partner's shoulders outlined dimly against the blurred window.

"Doggonit," protested Indigo. "I'm beginning to get goose pimples. What's out there in the rain you're so excited about?"

"Crowheart Ames just slid into that Mex joint," muttered Joe.

"Which proves he ain't got much taste," said Indigo. "I quit drinking raw alcohol some time back."

"Nuggins is in there, remember that?"

"No law against it, is they? Light the lamp, Joe, before I get separated from my status quo. Now who's cooking up trouble?"

Joe fumbled with the lamp. The wick glowed against his bronzed and handsome face. Excitement flickered in his eyes. Indigo groaned, for he knew the signs; Joe was slow to rouse, yet when his imagination and his temper were alike fired by chance events he became volcanic, he moved with a tremendous impatience and was as crafty as an Apache on the war trail. Indigo exploded very easily and was as quick to cool. Not Joe. There were no lengths to which he would not go, no distances he would not cover, hardly any risk he would not take in order to satisfy the awakened warrior in him.

"Once," he murmured, "when I was in Abilene—"

Indigo punched a pillow and began to protest. "Now listen, Joe, let's get some sleep. My mature judgment says I should get out of Terese prompt. I'm staying because I ain't got no sense. But I sure need sleep before I start following you from hell to supper. Le's—"

He interrupted himself, turning his waspish face toward the door. The stairway creaked, steps drummed irregularly down the hall and a door squealed. Someone entered the adjoining room; and through the paper-thin partition came the choked, terribly intense sound of a woman laboring with tragedy.

Joe's face drew tight and bleak. He had heard women cry before; crying from temper, from broken dreams, from those unfathomable impulses that neither he nor any other man could comprehend. Here, for the second time this eventful day, he was witness to a woman's heart being torn apart. And the sound tortured him until the room grew too small and the outrage smoldered like a forge fire. It rose and fell, weird and muffled. It died to the smallest suspiration and rose again to a pitch of frenzy. Joe paced the room and threw a haunted glance at Indigo.

"By God, Indigo, Terese is a hard county! What's that poor soul troubled with?"

Indigo reached for his cigarette papers, frowning heavily. "The more I see of these parts the better I'd like to be on the trail. Where you going?"

Joe had reached the end of his rope. He strode to the door. "I got to see if I can't help a mite. Hell, Indigo, nobody's got a right to stand back and listen to that!" He ducked into the gloom-ridden hall and went to the adjoining room. He thought he saw the shadows shifting strangely near the stair landing but he was so preoccupied that he violated a lifelong rule of look-and-see. He stood a moment by the woman's door, scarcely knowing what to do. He shook his head, raised his hand and drummed the panel lightly.

There was no answer. He knew there wouldn't be. A woman crying like that wouldn't hear anything. So, dropping his hand to the knob, he violated another rule of his life, as well as breaking an unwritten commandment of the land, and pushed the door before him. A deep-rooted sense of propriety caused him to tarry on the threshold. But when he saw the girl of the dance hall, Ray Chasteen, lying on the bed, her clothes rumpled and wet, he closed the door behind and broke the unendurable silence.

"I'm begging your pardon, ma'am. I ain't got a right in here. But—but I'm almost old enough to be your dad. And it hurts me to hear you cry like that."

She turned on the bed and rose. In the dim, fluttering lamplight all her features were softened and blurred. There was a golden radiance around her disheveled hair. She was dead white and the color of her eyes was quite lost in the upheaval of spirit. But to Joe she was a figure of beauty, wistful and crumpled beauty. His presence didn't frighten her, but it stopped her crying, it hardened her and brought a sullen resentment to her face. She threw back her head.

"I didn't ask you to come in. I don't want to see you. I don't want to see any man! You're all a pack of coyotes, you're all yellow and afraid of your lives. You slink around the strongest beast and do what he tells you to do! What right have *you* got to be proud of yourself! Oh, if I were a man tonight I'd kill!"

Joe dropped his head. "Yes, ma'am. I reckon you would. But you're not a man and so you can't. I guess I'm intruding. But I wanted to say that maybe I can help. Also I wanted to say that I will personally account for the man who killed Sam Trago. I will personally see to it. Just wanted to say that, ma'am."

It only roused her fury. "Go back to Praygood Nuggins or to Dead Card John and tell whichever of them you take orders from that you came up here to torment me! Tell them you found me crying. Crying! That will please them! But they will suffer. If there's no power on earth to make them pay, then there will be in the place they go. Get out. I don't trust you!"

Joe shook his head slowly. He straightened, a fine, soldierly figure. The dim light accentuated the silvering crust around his temples; shadows sank into the lines of his face and lay heavily against his eyes, making him appear weary. Yet nothing could obscure the kindly mellowed sympathy of that face. There was a quality about Joe Breedlove that, once known, was never forgotten. And because of it a thousand friends along his long trail had regretted his passing. It seemed to be that Joe, old in no sense of the word, appeared to people as a gallant figure against the sunset; a rugged and straightforward man, swept clean of youthful egotism and youthful intolerance. Life had sweetened him and the full savor of his serene, robust temper radiated outward and drew others to him swiftly and surely.

"I wish, ma'am, you'd look at me. Yeah, I know you're looking already. But you're not seeing me as I am, but as you figure I must be."

"Why should I trust you?" she asked, the anger slightly thinning.

"Well, men have trusted me, I reckon."

"Men? Why should I follow after fools?"

Joe drew a breath. His words made a resonant, musical echo in the room, beating against the slashing, battering note at the storm. "I'll ask you, then, to trust me as some women have trusted me."

Thunder crashed upon the town, shaking this frame structure like a rag. He saw the anger die, he saw her lips part but he couldn't hear what she whispered. And then her despairing cry filled the room. "They killed Sam because—because he was a good man!" Joe stepped forward, his arm raised. The girl's will gave out and she fell against him, the hot tears scalding his hand. And Joe held her up, murmuring the same small comforting words he would have used for a child; saying them over and over again until the very monotony seemed to soothe her.

"The boy is dead. But there'll be a man to pay me for that in the next forty-eight hours."

She drew back, drained of emotion, and she spoke with a weariness and a finality that Joe was to remember all the rest of the days of his life. "That won't bring Sam back to me."

"God bless you, ma'am. Now you're talking like a woman, and I'm only saying what any fool man would say. Still, the ledger's got to be balanced. And there'll be red ink in the book before tomorrow night's through. There's more killings to come out of this. Terese is set for a struggle. Ma'am, there are just two things good for a sore troubled spirit. One is sleep, which I've tried myself. And the other is prayer. I bid you good night." He turned his back to her abruptly, dreading to meet her eyes again; and he closed the door softly and groped back to his own room.

Indigo still sat on the bed, with a litter of cigarette butts around his feet. He looked to Joe out of red and sleepy and dubious orbs. "Well?"

Joe only shook his head.

Indigo started to fashion another smoke. Joe walked to the window and stared into the rain-lashed night, thoroughly buried with his thoughts. The door latch clicked, Indigo sprang from the bed with a warning grunt and reached for his gun. Joe swung. The door was wide and Dead Card John stood framed in the opening, seeming thinner and taller than before. Out of the turbulent, stormy night he had emerged without a crease or a spot on his black broadcloth suit; the marble pallor of his cheeks appeared more pronounced, a severe set expression—only such a fixity of features that a man of one particular profession could assume so well—was on them. And he looked directly at Joe, disregarding Indigo's poised arm.

"You were a dead man," said he, "when you opened that girl's door."

Joe's head dropped and rose. "I reckon you had a right to shoot me then. I was stepping over a tall fence—which ain't always a fault of mine. Lay back, Indigo. The gentleman carries his gun under his shoulder." Indigo relaxed; these two tall characters, so dissimilar in every outward respect, matched glances across the room. Joe went on, dropping into the lazy and musical drawl that, at times like these, hid the fermentation inside of him. "Thought I noticed something down that hall. Well, having heard what conversation passed, what's your opinion now?"

"I regard you as a friend," replied Dead Card John in the same level, frigid voice. "Don't let it worry you. I never ask a man's good opinion."

Joe nodded. "After our first meeting I would say you wasn't in the business of answering questions. Still, I reckon I'll ask if Sam Trago was a friend of yours."

"I never ask a man's good opinion," repeated Dead Card John with emphasis. "Trago shared the county's opinion of me, friend. I let Trago alone—I let his folks put a fence around a few acres of hard scrabble."

"And it's your territory up that way," mused Joe. "Which is to say that others may own it but your word goes."

Dead Card John said nothing.

Joe shifted the subject. "Ray Chasteen. It's a pretty name. I was wondering if they wasn't somebody near to her. Where's the girl's folks?"

For the first time Dead Card John permitted a trace of animation to escape through his eyes. "Ray Chasteen's mother, friend, is sleeping out yonder on a hill. Once she was the greatest singer in the West."

"What about her dad?" asked Joe, his head moving imperceptibly forward.

Dead Card John stood like a post. "She ain't known a dad since she was four."

Joe's sleepiness dropped. He moved nearer. "I'll ask another question, mister. How bad do you want Ox Bow?"

Indigo looked at his partner with an incredulous surprise. It wasn't like Joe to violate etiquette so flagrantly. Then he fastened his attention on Dead Card John with a greater intensity than he had thus far. But Dead Card John showed no resentment. "I'll expose my hand to you, friend. As long as Sam Trago lived I didn't want an inch of Ox Bow. Sam Trago never knew it, but I was behind him. And the man who tried to run Sam off would have had me to look at. But now, friend, I'm fighting for Ox Bow. Let it lay like that."

"Why should you be telling me?" asked Joe.

Dead Card John didn't answer the question directly. "You're nobody's fool, friend. You know what's going on hereabouts, don't you? I would lay a bet on it. I have never asked a favor of Terese. But if you'll side a piece with me tonight I'll show you something else."

"Why?" drawled Joe.

Dead Card John moved his shoulders. "You bought a hand in the deal I saw happen this afternoon. The ride will be about two miles."

Joe nodded. "Come on, Indigo."

"Meet me down the street by the stable," said Dead Card John and disappeared in the hall. Indigo groaned.

"Doggone it, Joe, there's a fine bear trap. Dark—raining like sixty—two miles out to some shanty full of leather scratchers. You ain't using good sense."

"The man's proud," said Joe.

"Hell, so'm I," grumbled Indigo. "But I—"

"He's proud," interrupted Joe. "It breaks his back to ask a favor. I'd say he ain't ever had to do any such asking recently. But he sure was putting in a call for help right now."

"I didn't hear no such words."

"No, but he was asking just the same. Come on, Indigo."

Indigo the fighter, Indigo the trouble-hunting bantam rooster, looked at the bed with mournful eyes and tried a last argument. "Ever strike you some peculiar he picked on total strangers for help? Why don't he get home talent? I like to sort around and find my own grief."

"Maybe strangers is the only help he can get. Come on."

"Oh, all right," said Indigo wearily. "I thought I was some hound for misfortune before I met you. But them days was like summer weather when I figure back. You got me worn to a thin shadow."

Joe was half down the hall. "Shucks, Indigo, you was nothing but skin and bones when I found you. The summer's made you seal fat."

Indigo's hot and personal protest punctuated the gloom. They crossed an empty lobby and let themselves into the rain-whipped night. Fewer lights burned in Terese; and those sent ragged beams across a flooded street. The partners beat against the wind, Joe in the lead. He heard a queer wailing down in the mud near by, an unearthly cater-wauling sound that suggested somebody gargling poison. Joe crouched at the mouth of an alley, hands touching a body. The mournful dirge grew more energetic.

"Who's this?" asked Joe.

"It's me—Snipe. Go 'way. I ain't fit to be talked to. Go on 'way."

"What's persuaded you to come out here and catch consumption?" Joe wanted to know.

"Sam's dead. Just found it out—gosh, I can't tell the old man that! I'm drunk, but I wish I was a heap drunker. What's to b'come of Ox Bow now? Hell, I ain't got nerve enough to go back home. Go 'way."

Joe tarried a moment. "Better let me boost you up—"

"Keep your paws off me!" protested the unhappy Ox Bow messenger. "A fine fandango it'll be."

The partners went on to the stable, got their horses and rode toward the street's end. Dead Card John waited in the driving rain for them and the trio traveled silently away from town, quartering across a dead black desert. Joe's sense of direction told him he headed approximately back up the afternoon trail, but he didn't get his exact bearings until he saw the desert narrow and squeeze between tall, precipitous shadows. And a light glimmered by the road. They were at the lonely tavern wherein drink had been refused them. They rode abreast it and halted; Dead Card John disappeared for a full minute's interval. He came back afoot, raising his words against the plunging elements.

"A man's in there to see me. If you've got stomach for eavesdropping go to the back door and come in the small room. It opens to the bar. You'll hear something."

"I practice deception because it's a crooked world," said Joe. "All right."

The partners left their horses standing on the lee side of the building and groped along the wall until they struck a door. It let them into a room dark and stagnant. But a point of light came through a remote keyhole and, guided by it, they reached that inner door opening upon the bar. Joe turned the knob with caution and left the door slightly ajar. The same barkeep slouched behind the mahogany; over at a table with a lamp between them sat Dead Card John and the county's sheriff, Crowheart Ames. The latter's hands were flat on the table, palms up. He was smiling as he asked Dead Card John a question.

"Where's all your men?"

"You know the answer to that," replied Dead Card John. "Nuggins has stolen part of them. The rest of them are no good to me—I've got no faith in any."

"Why blame me?" countered Crowheart Ames.

"You've been mighty polite to Nuggins lately, Crowheart."

"Got to make it appear as if I'm impartial, don't I? But you know how I stand. You know exactly."

Dead Card John's face was marked with lines, as if he held back some terrific temper. "Do I know? I'm not so sure, Crowheart. Listen. I made you. I took you out of that saloon and made you. Hear that? I kept you in office, Crowheart. And you licked my boots as long as you knew you were safe."

"Say, I don't care much about that kind of—"

"Shut up. You're a lickspittle. Been one all your life. You

stuck fast with me as long as I looked good. But you'd jump the traces in a minute if you thought Nuggins could take the power away from me. Now you don't know whether he or I'll get that ranch. And you want to be on the right side."

Crowheart struck the table with his fists. "I got to appear neutral, don't I? You know me better. Tell me a Nuggins man you want in jail. I'll put him there. Tell me what you want done, I'll do it. But you got to start slashing the whip on your boys. Slack reins won't do. I been hearing some growling. I'd be in a pretty mess, wouldn't I, sitting on the wrong side of the fence. You got to move fast. It ain't right, I don't help. I do help. The gate's wide open as far as Ox Bow is concerned. You get busy. I'll back you up with every legal trick there is. It's yours, John. Yours and a little cut for me. But you got to get busy. Now, I'll do what you say. Name it."

There was a wheedling, uneasy note in the man's voice. Dead Card John almost spat at him. "Well, why haven't you got Sam Trago's killer in jail? Why haven't you got posses out? You're trimming to the winds, Crowheart!"

"Tell me who killed him. I'll get the gent if you name him. Besides—" and Crowheart's words were heavily significant —"why raise a ruckus about that? It opens the ranch wide to all comers don't it? You get busy."

"Rube Mamerock isn't dead yet, Crowheart."

The sheriff nodded his head. "I'm leaving that to your judgment. Since when did you get religion?"

Dead Card John got up and turned. It was the signal for which Joe waited. He pushed into the room, glad to have this part of the deal over with. Crowheart kicked the chair from under him, growing red and excited. "Tricks, huh?"

"I practice deceit because it's a crooked world," said Joe. "I don't like it none, so I'll just clear myself by saying I heard most of what you said."

The sheriff shook his fist at Dead Card John. "You can't play me like that! Your boat's sinking. You know it. Dragging in strange alley cats ain't goin' to help none! I'll drive 'em out o' Terese faster'n hell!"

Dead Card John stared the sheriff into silence. "When I have to kill a man, Crowheart, I want witnesses to tell why I do it. You're about to follow Nuggins's kite. You figure there's where the money is. All right. Nuggins dies before he gets Ox Bow. Mark that, Crowheart. I'm the man who takes Ox Bow. And God help you if you guess wrong and cut me!"

Crowheart backed toward the door, his pug face set in a defiance not quite free from fear. He swept the partners up and down. "You're out of this quarrel, pilgrims. Better leave Terese behind. John, I ain't taking no war talk from you. I don't want to fight you. Get busy and I'll do my share. But don't ride me. You ain't so broad in the pants as you used to be." He backed into the darkness.

Dead Card John turned to Joe. "Friend, I'm obliged for your coming. Have a drink. I never ask a man to drink with me. You saw Crowheart's hand."

Joe and Indigo tipped their glasses solemnly while Dead Card John stood back, fingering the fob hanging from his vest. Joe faced the man, slightly smiling. "I'd say the next excitement was due about tomorrow night at the Ox Bow. Maybe you've got an invite?"

Dead Card John shook his head. "Rube Mamerock would cut off his hand before he took notice of me. But I will be there."

Joe reached into a coat pocket, raised his fist and dropped a half dozen of Ox Bow's leaden invitations on the bar. "One for yourself. Better bring some competent help with you."

Indigo stared in wonder at the shells. Dead Card John swept the room with his arm. "Once I had men who never left this place unless I told them. Where's my help now? I am obliged for the shells. I'll be there."

Joe nodded to Indigo; and both of them started for the front door. On the threshold Joe turned back with a last word. "I reckon we've seen everybody's hand in this deal but yours. Don't let that worry you none. I know what your hole card is."

"I doubt that, friend," replied Dead Card John somberly.

"It's a trick I learned when I was a kid—down in Abilene." He saw the man start toward him, eyes blazing against the white skin. But he pushed Indigo before him into the darkness. And in a moment they were riding back for Terese.

"He's asking for help," said Joe, bowing his face to the slantwise rain. "And he knows we're in on the deal."

"Who said so?" snapped Indigo. "I didn't hear no words to them sentiments."

"What do you figure I gave him the slugs for, Indigo?"

"Yeah? Say, when did you get them anyhow?"

"Out of that Ox Bow man's pocket, when he was wallering in the mud. Don't chew your words so bad, Indigo."

"More pious robbery!" howled Indigo. "My, this stinks. So we're helping a notorious son-of-a-gun steal a ranch. Joe, you're crazy! You're plumb lunatic. How far have I got to singe my whiskers in this mess? I don't get you a-tall."

"It's this fellow Dead Card John against Praygood Nuggins. Somebody's got to drop."

"What difference does it make?" asked Indigo, thoroughly roused. "They're both so crooked a snake'd break his back trying to foller their shadows. Let 'em drop. It can't be done —said stealing—unless this Rube Mamerock's plugged. And further unless one bunch wipes out the other bunch. And still further unless they's a lot of corruption in holding the property from rightful heirs. You mean to tell me you deliberately aim to dirty up your reppitation with this? Say—!"

"If Rube Mamerock dies, it won't be by Dead Card John's bullet," stated Joe. "I'm laying all my spare cash on that. But if the old duck does die and there's a fight for the outfit, then Nuggins has got the drop on Dead Card John. That's what this skate Al was doing up at that roadside honkytonk tonight when we first rode through. He's Nuggins' way of tinkering with John's riders. Yeah. Dead Card John is blame' near licked now."

"Let him get licked. You and me had better eat breakfast a long ways south of Terese."

"We eat barbecued meat at the Ox Bow tomorrow night, Indigo. And if trouble starts we're standing beside Dead Card John. Sleep on it. I know what his hole card is. It's a good card."

Indigo punctured the gusty, wet night with the sulfuric outpourings of a ridden soul. They came to Terese again and slept.

CHAPTER 4

Unless a man wished to break his neck in trying to descend the rear bluffs, there was but one entrance to the Ox Bow home quarters and that turned from the Terese trail and crossed the river at the trembling and narrow wood bridge. When the partners arrived at the turn-off, lanterns made a flickering and uncertain cluster in the very middle of that bridge. They embarked upon it single-file; the river, swollen by the steady rains, boiled a foot beneath the planking and the whole structure swayed as if it were a raft. It gave Indigo a very queer feeling in the pit of his stomach; he was no sailor and he disliked leaving the firm underfooting of the land.

"It's like the rest of Terese," he grumbled, "held together

by rotten string. This thing ain't apt to be here by morning if it keeps on raining. Hustle on, Joe, before she buckles."

Other travelers came behind, likewise in single file, and the bridge shook with each hoofbeat. Midway, lanterns flared against Joe's face; he was challenged by a pair of slickered cowhands. "Tickets, gents." Joe produced the slugs and the pair gave the leaden invitations a severe, close inspection. The lanterns rose again and fell more fully upon the partners. The nearest of the bridge guardians spoke dubiously. "Strangers here?"

"Yeah. But your messenger struck up a close friendship with us last night."

"I reckon," was the spokesman's dry answer. "Most of Terese was Snipe's friends about then. How in hell—?"

The other cowpuncher ended this. "Let 'im pass. He's got an invite. An invite is an invite."

"What would stop some unasked gent from manufacturing his own invite?" asked the curious Joe.

"It's been tried before," was the laconic answer. "The results ain't usually fatal, but they're painful. Pass on, stable your brutes and assume total freedom of the premises. But how in hell—?"

The partners moved away, hearing the brace of punchers pass dire words concerning Snipe. "That's about the ninth mistake Snipe made. The old man'll sure kill the weasely little runt if he ever shows up here again. Ain't had good sense at no time. We better start refusing some of these invites. Rube never meant 'em to get scattered around like handbills."

"An invite is an invite," argued the other. "Anybody that shows one here gets acrost the bridge, if it's a Chinese, sheepherder or spaniel dog. You know Rube never dishonors his invites. That damn' Snipe had better keep heading away from Terese, no mistake. Invites, gents."

The partners went on, reaching an enormous open shed. More lanterns confronted them and roustabouts led away their horses. They ducked around a dark corner of the house, climbed the steps and were again halted by everpresent Ox Bow men. "Guns, gents."

Joe surrendered his own without argument and saw it hung on a peg beside twenty others. But Indigo was reluctant, and only a prod of Joe's thumb stilled his protest. "What kind of a party is this, anyhow? Without my gun I feel sorter naked, and some giddy."

The custodian of lethal hardware stabbed his thumb toward a corner of the room. "There's a keg over there with the head knocked out. Drop a dipper into it, fellow, and

95

you'll either recover from said giddy feeling or you'll get so worse it won't make no difference."

They strolled into a room as immense as a barn. Oak beams stretched across it, two stories high; a dozen bracketed lamps flooded the place with light. At one end a fireplace, wider and more massive than the partners had ever seen, was choked with blazing logs. Doors opened from this room on three sides and the partners had a partial view of long rows of tables set for a feast. Already a substantial gathering filled the ranch house. Men arrived, gave up their guns, and circled past the welcoming kegs; men drifted casually through the room, singly and in pairs; they clustered in groups, the smoke of their pipes spiraling to the beams. Joe took a sparing drink, but Indigo plunged a tin cup into the very bowels of the barrel and drew it back dripping full. He drank it like water and hung his cheerless, brooding face over the open barrel's mouth.

"I rise to remark this Mamerock fellow ain't niggardly in no proportions. Joe, what makes a keg full of liquor look so much better than the same amount in bottles? It just makes me thirsty. You could drive a herd through this joint without scraping paint."

"Hit that keg easy," warned Joe. "We got a good use for temperance tonight."

Indigo threw an exasperated stare at his partner and surrendered the cup. "I thought there'd be some sort of catch. Joe, if I found a fifty-pound nugget lying on the prairie I'd prob'ly have two busted arms and couldn't pick it up. Or I'd go color blind and pass it by for a plain rock."

They ambled toward the fireplace. There was a white-haired man standing with his back to the flames, a powerful figure overladen with fat and crippled and twisted by an apparent rheumatism. Others flanked him and presently Joe heard his name called. It was Rube Mamerock. Joe watched the Ox Bow owner's shaky fingers struggling with a match and his sympathy, never far below the surface, was instantly enlisted. All men had to die, but it was a pity they couldn't go out before they felt the helplessness of old age. Here was one who had been a tremendous fighter. And now the wolves were snapping at his heels and he had his back to the wall; a man who, on the eve of an anniversary, had a gray and discouraged and troubled look upon his cheeks. The white head bobbed up and down in answer to a low spoken comment.

"You boys know I been a good neighbor," Joe heard him say. "I never set a heavy hand on my friends. I've had a good time living. What more can anybody ask? Smoke and.

drink and eat hearty. It's a cold night out. Reminds me of seven years ago. The year of the big drive north. Keep warm, boys. Like to see you enjoy yourselves. Like to have it feel like old times. Old-timers go pretty fast. This is the last fandango Rube Mamerock ever gives at Ox Bow."

"Who killed the boy, Rube?"

Mamerock's eyes flared; and as quickly lost the momentary anger. "God knows. But if I was ten years younger I'd rip Terése upside down and put the fear of death in some certain hearts. They know they got me hamstrung. Just waiting now to rip open my neck. With Sam gone they won't have to wait long. Only, they better do it quick. I ain't useless complete."

The wolves, Joe repeated to himself, were snapping at the old man's heels. And, hearing a sudden hush cross the room, he turned toward the door. The wolves were growing braver. Praygood Nuggins stood on the threshold, and beside him was the henchman, Al. Nuggins carried himself as erect as a soldier, his stern eyes and thin compressed lips half hidden by the dripping hat and the flowing yellow mustache. He looked directly at Rube Mamerock and started toward the old man, Al trailing. Praygood Nuggins looked sidewise and jerked his hand. Al retreated, exactly as a dog might have been ordered home. In the adjoining room a man laughed boisterously, the sound jarring the almost complete silence here.

Nuggins paused in front of Mamerock, dipping his head with exact courtesy. "I am obliged for your kind invitation. It's the first time you have honored me. I reckon folks soften some as they get old. I thank you kindly."

Mamerock was as gray as cold wood ashes. He matched Nuggins's bow and Nuggins's severe politeness. "An invite is the same as my word, sir. I will not deny it, nor never have. You are on Ox Bow premises for the first time. I bid you enjoy yourself."

"I'm obliged," drawled Nuggins. "I sure trust that though it's the first time it won't be the last."

Some of Mamerock's dying vigor colored his eyes. "The evening is apt to settle that, Mr. Nuggins."

Nuggins wheeled and made for the whisky kegs. Joe saw the man barely wet his lips on the dipper and retreat through the door again. Five swart Mexicans filed into a corner and fiddled with their guitars; the place hummed with a stirring, vivid music, a puncher came out of the dining room and shouted, "Come and get it!" The crowd shifted. Crowheart Ames entered the place and alone of the guests forbore checking his gun. Behind him ranged a compact group of punchers, seeming more or less attached to him. His pug face bowed low to the whisky kegs and he saluted Rube Mamerock jovially. The Ox Bow owner nodded and walked away from the fire, followed by others eager to precede him. Ray Chasteen was on the threshold.

"Pretty," breathed Indigo. "Sorrow becomes that gal. Pretty, by Jupiter."

Rube Mamerock's awkward arms folded around her and Rube's heavy voice soared above the music. "God bless you, daughter, for coming to an old man's last fandango." Ray Chasteen's eyes flashed in the light and Rube, holding her arm with a fatherly gallantry, led her away from the men. The two of them disappeared in some other part of the house.

"Daughter?" grunted Indigo, following Joe into the dining room. "This Dead Card John jasper said she didn't know no dad."

"A figure of speech," drawled Joe. "She ain't his daughter, but he wishes she was. And mebbe she might have been a daughter by will, if she'd married this Sam Trago. Look around yourself, Indigo. You'll never see another gathering where they's so many broken hearts and so many slant-eyed gents with itching fingers."

"Beans," muttered Indigo, seizing a plate. Great haunches of beef, barbecued to a golden, steaming bronze lay on mammoth platters; tall crocks of beans, unearthed from a twenty-four-hour baking beneath a coal-heaped grave, studded the long tables. The Ox Bow doctor bustled in with smutted pots of coffee, a glum and unapproachable figure within all this joviality. The room filled, drawn by an incense that surpassed all the aromatic spices of the Indies. Cattleland loved this sort of provender. Indigo helped himself, not scorning to use force and deception in beating another man to the carving knife and the ladle; for Indigo was one whose thoughts were never scattered over a variety of subjects at the same time. When he fought he did so to the utter exclusion of everything else. And when he went to the trenchers it was with the same single-minded intensity that characterized his trouble-checkered career.

Not for Indigo was the subtle weaving of treachery and defiance within Rube Mamerock's ranch house. But Joe, eating thoughtfully, stood back against a wall and saw what most men missed. Joe was a natural born spectator of life; he loved to weigh and judge men from their speech and from the impress of emotion upon their faces. One by one he checked them over, his serene blue eyes resting above the rim of his coffee cup. He saw the more substantial of them

—the old-timers and the ranch owners—imperceptibly draw to themselves. And he knew they would support Rube Mamerock because they were his kind. They would back Rube by the weight of their numbers.

Elsewhere, the same sort of division went on. Ranch hands of particular outfits stood side by side; groups of young bucks heady with drink; and two small bunches of men who held strictly aloof from each other and said very little. Rube's own punchers slouched at odd angles of the place and upon these Joe fastened his penetrating philosopher's eye. Loyalty to an outfit was a powerful thing; still, threat and bribery were almost as powerful. Joe looked into the depths of his cup and shook his head. Rube Mamerock's kingdom was crumbling.

Excitement laid its suppressing hand over the room. He saw it etched upon every face. He saw it in the unconscious snapping of jaw muscles, in swift and turning glances, and the short, cautious exchange of words here and there. Every one of them knew a showdown to be approaching. Even Rube Mamerock, who was out of sight in this rambling house, knew it. Joe laid down his cup and turned to Indigo who rested against the wall in the manner of a thoroughly gorged python.

"Let's amble, Indigo."

They passed into the main room. Only a few were here. But there was one newcomer. Dead Card John stood alone in a remote corner, dressed in the same faultless black and white. His severe ivory-colored face made a queer outline in the shadows. His eyes caught a beam of light and the flash of that impact was like the reflection of sun on ice. He saw the partners, giving no sign of recognition.

Indigo bristled a bit, but Joe pushed him toward the whisky barrels. "Fortify yourself, Indigo."

Indigo stared at his partner, astonished. "What's coming off here?"

"Warm up. It's chilly outside and that's where we're going for a spell."

Indigo hooked his chin over the keg's rim, hypnotized by the amber depths. "A pretty sight," he muttered. He took a cup and swashed it along the surface of the whisky much as a small boy would run his hand across a pool of water. He drank soundly and hitched up his pants, glaring at the distant Dead Card John with the pale light of hostility flickering in his green orbs. "Let nobody tromp on my instincks," said he.

They went past the checked guns, Joe scanning the rows of massed artillery with intent interest; they stepped into the night and rounded a corner of the house. The rain beat slantwise out of a dead black sky; the wind ripped across the open desert, shrilling at the touch of corral post and building eaves. They heard the river splashing against its sandy banks, they heard a high-pitched phrase beating across the blackness. A single lantern weaved out there on the bridge. The lights around the sheds were fewer and dimmer. Indigo and Joe crouched against the wall of the house.

"Now you're up to some of that Eyetalian embroidery again," complained Indigo, raising his voice.

"Come on—we're going to see how that dry channel back of the house looks."

They stumbled across the uneven ground, avoiding the sheds. Within its shelter they saw four men crouched beneath a lantern and another figure standing just beyond its revealing rays. Fifty yards farther they came to the margin of the abandoned river channel. This night it sighed and rumbled to the overflow. The abraded banks were crumbling, the scouring side eddies rose above and poured across the level land on which the partners stood.

Joe explored along the edge gingerly. "Nobody's coming to the fandango from this way tonight, Indigo."

"Yeah. Well, when you're through with all them natural observations le's get to cover. I'm dripping like a faucet."

"We slide around toward the bridge next. Don't shout so loud."

They circled back, traversing unfamiliar ground. Light poured out of the ranch-house windows and a commotion rose by the front door. The partners halted. Around the corner veered a lantern, held high over four men struggling with a fifth. The fifth was howling like a lone wolf in the hills; he bucked, broke loose and created havoc, the tenor of his speech scandalously profane. They caught him again and rushed him forward to what, in the advancing light, appeared to be a root house depressed almost level with the earth. One of the party drew open the slanting doors and the protesting individual was hurled through. The door closed, a last weird howl beating out of the depths.

"First drunk," said one of the party. "That celler will be crawling with 'em afore morning." They disappeared around the house corner.

The partners made a cautious detour of the lights, quartering against the wind. The temper of the storm rose steadily. A sage stalk struck Joe, a shrill yell slid by and they saw a second lantern waving crazily in the night, borne toward the bridge by a stumbling figure. Joe muttered "Hurry up," and aimed in that direction. They arrived near the bridge end as the guard of the structure drew landward to meet the man approaching. Neither of the partners heard anything of the moment's parley but, watching the lanterns closely, Joe noticed the erstwhile guard retreating toward shelter while the new man walked out upon the weaving structure.

"Hear that water grumbling," said Indigo. "This bridge won't stick, Joe. The guy ought to get off it."

"He will in a minute," replied Joe. "But he's got particular business right now. Watch."

The guard's lantern dipped thrice as if in signal; then the light of it winked out.

"Wind snuffed it for him," said Indigo.

"No, he's hiding it inside his coat. We got to get closer to this shebang. Here's the guard rail. Flat on your stomach, Indigo. Hug the under side of these planks."

"Hell!" exploded Indigo. "I'm wet enough now."

Horses drummed along the bridge, a man ran behind. Joe looked around and up from his shelter to see a point of light seeping out from the guard's coat. Those in the saddle were halted. Whether they were two or six Joe couldn't tell, but he heard them talking.

"Where's the rest?" asked the guard. "Better get the whole bunch over now. If she keeps rising the bridge'll wash down the crick."

"Nuggins give orders. Just us boys to hang around here, out of sight. The main bunch waits till he sends for 'em."

"They mebbe won't be able to cross in another hour," persisted the bridge tender.

"You go argue with Nuggins if you want. I aim to keep my health, so I'm obeying directions. How about us going into the sheds?"

"Nope. You wouldn't be welcome. Go to the barn."

The partners waited until the bridge end was deserted again before rising from their concealment. Indigo's temper was ragged and his sense of pride had been assaulted by this burrowing into the mud. He said so in blunt, gloomy words. "And I'm too old a hand, Joe, to take chances with rheumatics any more. This is a hell of a place for you and me. Le's ride."

"Let's go back and get a drink."

"Well—that ain't such a bad suggestion either."

They raised their shoulders against the stinging rain and retreated for the house. Ten yards from the door they were met by another squad of semi-sober men conveying a drunk to the root cellar. Praygood Nuggins stepped after them and turned into the darkness. Joe laid a detaining hand across Indigo's arm. One flat and angry word cut over the noisy air. A cry of pain came hard after it and presently Nuggins reappeared on the threshold of the house and went inside. But somebody out in the darkness was cursing blackly. The partners entered and went quickly toward the whisky kegs.

In the space of time the two had been wandering around in the storm a change had come over the crowd. More exactly it was a tightening of the nervous excitement already existing. The room was warm, smoke lifted in clouds, thick enough to eddy and swirl behind the moving bodies. Drink touched them all and the fast, thrumming music of the Mexican guitars stirred the blood. Even the cool-tempered Joe felt himself swayed by it, felt a turn to recklessness. Eyes about him were hard and bright; men were watching each other with a telltale caution.

Dead Card John stood in the same corner, still alone and still maintaining the marble severity of his face. But his attention was fixed upon Praygood Nuggins across the room and Nuggins, erect and grim, returned the glance. This man's features were half hidden by the low-setting hat and the drooping yellow mustache. All that could be seen with any degree of clearness was the bold nose and the angular, slanting eyes. He appeared to be standing guard, such was the fixity of his muscles and the unvarying cast of his cheeks. And the henchman Al stood a few paces removed in a similar posture though he could not erase the slack and cynical grin from his face.

Joe noted that other men, some of them Ox Bow hands, seemed too casual as they draped themselves on Nuggins's side of the place.

Though the talk rolled on and the music drummed along the rafters, all men were waiting. Waiting for that certain yet unguessable move that would set fire to this pile of tinder. Alone of the crowd, Rube Mamerock seemed unmoved. He had taken a seat by the fireplace, hands folded over his paunch. And there was an air of weary, discouraged sadness about him that tugged at Joe's heart. Mamerock's race was run. He had made his mark, built up his empire. Now, with the specter of death casting a long, long shadow before him he saw the forthcoming dissolution of all that he had labored to gain. With the passing of Sam Trago there had also passed his last hope of leaving the Ox Bow intact. His chin dropped to his chest and the silver hair gleamed in the light. He was beaten.

Dead Card John moved away from his corner, approaching Rube Mamerock. And such was the growing tension that the talk stumbled and fell to a small murmuring. All the henchmen shifted and looked toward Praygood Nuggins; but the latter never stirred. His eyes were fixed upon Dead Card John with a sharpness that photographed every ripple of expression on the latter's graven face. Dead Card John bent over Mamerock, lips barely moving. Mamerock shook his head, not looking up. But Dead Card John bent lower, speaking again, the ivory pallor giving way to a taint of red. Mamerock reared back and stared fully at Dead Card John for long moments. Complete silence came to that room, the guitars stopped and the singing of the fire through the oak wood made a queer melody against the rumble of the storm. Mamerock's head fell and rose. He hoisted himself from the chair, pointing to an inner door, the meanwhile looking about him.

"Play up," said he to the musicians. "I don't expect to hear much music by-and-by. Play up, boys." And he waved his hand around the room. "Friends, if you'd please an old-timer, hit those kegs and look as if you were enjoying yourselves. Rube never spread a poor fandango yet and I don't want it said the last one was dull." He opened the designated door, let Dead Card John and himself into another room, and closed the portal behind.

Still Praygood Nuggins kept his exact place, his flinty and angular cheeks turned to the recently closed door. For once the henchman Al's face was bereft of its slack grin. The man shuffled nervously to the kegs and drank, setting up an example that struck the crowd appropriately. The tension snapped, talk soared to the dark beams, the whisky kegs were plumbed to the bottom. A brace of Ox Bow men rolled in a fresh vessel and cut away the top. One elderly rancher with a gloss-black beard and a steel eye raised the dipper to the room and spoke resoundingly. "God bless old Rube. God condemn the man who sets his loop for the Ox Bow!"

The room filled with a roar. Yet Joe, measuring the warmth of that sentiment's approval marked it down that it lasted only a moment and was followed by an immediate shifting and gathering of groups. The old-timers were with Rube, heart and soul. But Joe plainly saw they feared Praygood Nuggins. The latter gave no notice to the toast, a thing ominous and unsettling to the onlookers. Individuals began idling toward the gun guardian. Al was at the front entrance, trying to catch Nuggins's attention. He caught it finally and raised himself to his toes as if to gain some certain consent. Joe saw Nuggins's head flick to one side in a quick negation.

The silver-haired partner dwelt thoughtfully upon this for a bare instant and spoke into Indigo's ear. "Inch toward the way out. Easy."

Unexpectedly, Crowheart Ames barred their path. His great chest expanded and he shoved his bulldog chin into Joe's face, speaking with a subdued belligerence.

"Where you going?"

Joe was suddenly cold and unfriendly. "It won't pay you to stand there long, Mister Ames."

"Keep your fingers out of this pie," warned the sheriff. Joe saw the man's pupils dilate.

"Get out of my way," drawled Joe. "I'm playing a waiting game—like you. Only I don't bluff. Step aside."

Ames moved back a pace and turned his shoulders. The partners cruised the width of the room, skirted the guns and stopped abreast of Al. The Nuggins henchman flashed a suspicious glance from one to the other and put his back to the wall like a balky horse. Indigo's pale orbs slowly turned to green and he looked at Al with a thoughtful mayhem printed upon his furrowed, waspish cheeks. Al started to say something and stopped, attention snapping into the room. Talk ceased, as if the bottom had dropped from the ranch house, and carried the crowd with it.

Indigo muttered, "Look there," and Joe turned upon his heels.

Rube Mamerock had returned to the fireplace. Dead Card John stood to one side of him and the girl, hidden all the evening, rested on the other. Something had happened to Rube in the brief intermission, something had taken twenty years from his face. He confronted the crowd, shoulders squared, the haunted, discouraged look gone from his eyes. He wasn't smiling, but there was a confidence or relief present that had not been there before. He swept the gathering, man and man, lingering a little on the soldierly figure of Praygood Nuggins. His head ducked, as if he had confirmed a belief. He raised his hand.

"Friends," said he, voice filling the room, "I have got an important message for you. I am going to make an oral will. I want every man here to testify to my words. I am about to do a duty that has troubled me, sleeping and waking, more than twenty years. I had it settled once. Then my plans was knocked aside. Mebbe God knows best. Listen very carefully. I am passing on Ox Bow to other hands."

The heavy and oppressive hand of silence squeezed the crowd like the jaws of a vise. Joe heard Al breathing asthmatically. As for himself, he rubbed his hands together and found the palms damp with sweat. Mamerock laid a hand on the girl's shoulder and continued.

"When I left Texas better than fifty seasons back, I cut all traces from my family. They're all dead and gone these many years. I know of ary kin. But there was two people in Terese I loved like son and daughter. I waited some years for Sam Trago to grow up. Sam was broad shouldered, he had a level head, and I knew blamed well Ox Bow would never suffer under his hands. I meant to will the ranch to Sam. I—"

He halted, and the crowd saw a sight they had never seen before. Rube Mamerock's cheeks were wet. Ray Chasteen held to him, her head high and proud, eyes burning like dark jewels against her white skin. Joe muttered a savage phrase to Indigo, "She can't cry no more, the poor girl."

"I figured I'd kept my intentions a secret," proceeded Rube Mamerock, catching hold of himself. "But the wolves found it out, or guessed it. So Sam died. And when he died my hopes died, too. It was to be Sam's ranch—and Ray Chasteen's. I wish I had a son like Sam and a daughter like Ray. The wolves figured they had me hamstrung. Up till ten minutes ago I guessed I was. But I have just been made aware of a fact which changes my ideas." He turned to the girl. "Daughter, I ain't at liberty to tell you anything. But what I say now I want you to follow and believe, trusting to old Rube Mamerock's judgment. Also trusting in what he tells you to do." With that he faced the crowd once more, chest spreading out with an immense intake of air. And his words rolled along the dead silent room with a booming, resonant solemnity.

"I, Rube Mamerock, being more or less sound of body and entirely clear and sane of mind, do hereby will, bequeath and freely give to Ray Chasteen the Ox Bow Ranch, with all its acres, buildings of whatever kind or nature, and all stock ranging upon it, and all vehicles and tools and furniture and gear, and all rights that go with the ranch, as well as every dollar I have in the various banks of this county and state, together with every interest I possess in other institutions and every share of stock to be found in my strongbox in the office. It is my plain will and intent to give everything I own to Ray Chasteen from the date of my death, regardless of whatever lack of legal language in this oral will. I want no such omission of lawyer phrases to defeat this disposition and I call upon every witness here tonight to make a good note of what I have said."

A tremendous escape of breath passed from the crowd, as if each man had himself delivered the speech and now wanted air. Boots shuffled, a murmuring rose. But Rube was not yet through and he waved his hand to still them.

"The wolves won't be satisfied. They'll figure to wrestle the Ox Bow away from a woman's hands. I have got a loyal outfit, but since old Rube's about done, I'll say that there's some of my men not to be trusted. In this room tonight are folks waiting—just waiting. I've fought those gents to a standstill while I lived. I am leaving a good fighter to take care of 'em now. The man I mention is one I always distrusted. Here and now I offer him an apology and I wish you all to testify I freely give him my confidence and trust. In order that Ray Chasteen's right to Ox Bow may be protected and defended, I hereby appoint as sole executor and administrator—"

He paused, shrewdly creating a suspense that none of them would forget. It was Rube Mamerock's last scene, his last fight, and he built up at this moment a climax that was to be a memorable chapter in Terese. Even the girl looked at him in wonder. Praygood Nuggins seemed to be a statue chiseled against the wall.

"—I appoint Dead Card John. And now I can die with some amount of security. Daughter, I will take you back—"

Not a sound escaped the crowd until Mamerock and the girl had disappeared in another room and the door was closed behind them. Dead Card John, at once the target of every eye, moved to the fireplace and stood with his back to it. Joe marveled at the man's cold, cast-iron courage. For Dead Card John surveyed a hostile assemblage with the same inscrutable, unrevealing glance he would have given to a hand of cards at a poker table. If the man had any outright supporters present Joe was not aware of them. On the contrary, he confronted an implacable enemy in Praygood Nuggins, with all the apparent aid Nuggins could muster within the space of a short word. He also had little to hope from the loyal Ox Bow hands or the old-timers. His reputation was behind him, his coldness repelled, and it was quite obvious to Joe that the crowd suspected he had somehow brought pressure upon Rube Mamerock, or had tricked the veteran.

He squared his thin shoulders and broke the long silence, speaking in a droning, emotionless manner sounding for all the world like an announcer at a gambling table. "You may believe it or not, gentlemen, but I wish to say that when the time comes for me to act in accordance with Rube's wishes I shall do so to the very letter. You gentlemen know my reputation. It will not agree with most of you. But you also know I have made it a policy to keep my word in Terese, good or bad. I give it now that Ray Chasteen shall receive every inch and penny of her estate."

Gradually, the crowd broke ranks and began a slow shifting, the talk rising from a subdued humming to an excited clatter. Crowheart Ames had one elbow on the whisky barrel, plunged in a study. Once he looked to Dead Card John and shifted the gaze to Praygood Nuggins. And it appeared to Joe that the sheriff was weighing his own chances of profit between those two antagonists. But Joe kept his attention riveted to Praygood Nuggins. And by-and-by he saw the man's chin drop toward Al. Al wheeled instantly and ducked into the storm. Joe prodded Indigo with a sharp elbow and ran down the steps, circling the corner of the house. Indigo stumbled in pursuit.

"Now what? Sa-ay, Joe, I ain't going to get any more goose pimples for anybody. What's up?"

"Horses, ropes. We're going to pull that bridge off its pins before the rest of Nuggins's sagebrush pirates cross. If these stable dudes make any shout, belt 'em in the stomach—"

The partners ducked under the shed and into the lantern light, arousing a quartet of Ox Bow men from a friendly game of pitch. The sight of them, plunging in from the storm, roused a quick alarm; nor did Indigo's thin embattled face tend to soothe them.

Joe swept the lantern up from the ground with a gruff explanation. "We're after our brutes. Come along, Indigo." And the partners raced down the shed.

An angry protest followed them. "Wait a minute—cut that out. I'll boost out all ponies here. Hey, hold on!"

But the partners were already in the saddle, swinging away. Joe dropped the lantern, the light guttered and died, a stream of profanity followed them. They rode side by side, untying their ropes; they reined in at the bridge end and dropped to the sodden earth. Joe took both ropes and walked out on the bridge until his exploring arm touched an upright post supporting the handrail. He dropped to his stomach, leaning far down toward the boiling current, made a quick tie with one rope and repeated the operation a few yards farther along with the remaining rope. Indigo, waiting in the saddle, took up the slack. Joe ran to his horse, mounted and gave the signal.

"They're comin' into it. Hear? All right, out she goes."

The planking threw out the sound of the advancing Nuggins crowd. The partners put a cautious strain on the ropes. "Out she goes," repeated Joe. Nails screamed, Joe's horse crouched for a harder pull. The bridge, warped and weakened by long years of traffic, held for a stubborn moment and then gave. The near end collapsed, planks snapped and dropped into the rushing stream.

Over the drumming beat of the rain sailed a warning cry. A gun flashed in the utter blackness. Joe's rope went slack. Indigo howled defiantly across the river and began to curse out of pure pleasure. The bridge, bereft of its underpinning at the near shore, collapsed section by section and they heard the tempestuous waters carrying it away. Both ropes were taut again, fouled in the driftwood downstream.

"She's out," said Joe. "Let the ropes go. We got business some place else."

"Say, I put in a lot of labor on my string," grumbled Indigo. "I want it—"

Another gunshot broke the galloping tempo of the storm, coming from the house. "Let it go!" shouted Joe. "Trouble back there."

The partners rode to the ranch door, dropped to the steps and ran inside. The crowd was bunched at the far end of the room. The door through which Mamerock last had passed swung wide. Somebody shouted, "He ain't in here. Look at the office." Ox Bow hands turned from the fringe of the crowd and slid into the dining room, Joe and Indigo close on their heels. Another door gave way. Cold air struck them in the face as they followed Ox Bow men into Rube Mamerock's office. More men spilled through from an opposite entrance, Dead Card John foremost. And the excited, threatening talk was damped at the raise of his arm.

Rube Mamerock was on his knees, between desk and chair, head lying on the desk's top. He had his back to the window and it seemed he was praying; but Dead Card John stepped up and ran one hand down the old man's coat to indicate a bullet hole. Then his long, tapering fingers slid inside the coat and touched the old man's chest. He stepped back, nodding. Mamerock was dead.

Crowheart Ames pointed accusingly at the window. "Glass splintered. Somebody shot him from outside." His fist doubled and his bulldog face shot out in the direction of the partners. "Where was you then? I saw you mooching out of the door!"

"You'll find our guns checked with the others," drawled Joe. "And I reckon we can account for our acts the last few minutes. Instead of standing here why don't you take a look outside by the window?"

Ray Chasteen fought through the ranks crying, "Let me

get in—let me get in!" Dead Card John turned and threw out both arms to stop her, but she knocked them aside and dropped in a heap by the dead Mamerock.

Joe averted his face and his eyes, passing across Dead Card John's marble countenance, saw terrific pain struggling to come through the ivory mask. "Let's get out of here," he suggested and led the way back to the main room.

One man had never left this room. Through all the excitement and the shifting of the crowd, Praygood Nuggins remained in the same spot near the wall. Still, he had improved 'the interval, for he wore his gun. The partners struck directly for the hall and the custodian of the artillery. The man was gone; Joe took his weapon from the wall and buckled it to him, blue eyes narrowing at the sight of Crowheart Ames's steady inspection. Indigo claimed his piece with a snort of satisfaction. "It was against my principles to undress in the first place. Just catch me doing it again."

The two of them stepped aside. They had started a rush. Every man in the place felt the spur of fear, and although Crowheart Ames yelled a command to stay away from the hardware, none paid him attention. For a moment it seemed to Joe the long anticipated fight would burst forth in that sullen jam of men struggling for their weapons. Nuggins and the sheriff were swapping some kind of a signal across the room; Ox Bow punchers were collecting in a corner by themselves for a bitter and subdued family discussion. But the old-timers, the backbone and the bulk of the crowd seemed to drift and gather around Crowheart Ames. The sheriff's red face grew wrinkled; he scooped a dipper of whisky from the keg and downed it recklessly. One rash, headlong challenge emerged from the Ox Bow bunch. "Well, here he is. Le's settle this thing for good!"

"Now," whispered Indigo, "this is where we ought to be some place else. What diff'rence does it make who steals the ranch? Ain't it plain both sides is robbers? Don't you believe nothing what this Dead Johnny gent says. And when you takes his part of the quarrel you're sure on the losing side. Look at 'em sifting toward this Nuggins buzzard."

Dead Card John came in, looked about him; and he saw that the crisis, long threatening, had come. He squared his thin shoulders.

"Gentlemen, I am the administrator of this estate. Ray Chasteen owns it. I ask every man who believes her entitled to it to stand beside me." So far the words were lifeless; and perhaps the man understood he made no friends,

109

for he turned until he confronted Praygood Nuggins and a controlled and bitter fury erupted. "Now, you damned dog, I'll call your bet! What are you going to do about it?"

"You worked it very well, John," said Nuggins. "But it won't last a minute. You can't hide behind a woman's petticoat."

"What do you propose to do?" snapped Dead Card John.

Nuggins ducked his stetson toward the old-timers ranged around the sheriff. "You boys are of a mind to see the girl gets her just dues, I reckon. I ain't bucking you none. But I don't propose to be put off the track either. What's Ray Chasteen to Mamerock? How does it happen our friend John and the lady is hooked together on the deal? You all know Rube Mamerock never had no truck with John. It ain't human nature to change so sudden without some sort of nigger in the woodpile. How long do any of you suppose the girl would hold Ox Bow with him in possession? How long do any of you figure she could run it, even if she got it away from him? Ox Bow's a man's ranch. I don't aim to fight a woman. Don't aim to get the county set against me. Ox Bow is worth something. I'll pay the girl a fair sum. More than it'd be worth ten months after she tried to run it." He met Dead Card John's challenge, his slanting eyes lifted against the light. "I'll tell you what I'm going to do, John. I'm having forty riders across the bridge in three minutes. And they'll rake hell out of you if it's your mind to put up a fight! I'm buying Ox Bow!"

"Excuse a stranger for buttin' in," drawled Joe Breedlove, "but I misdoubt you'll have any forty helpers across the river short of two days. The bridge is out. Me and my friend pulled it out. Old trooper, you'll have to do your scrapping with what men you got here and now."

"Who are you?" challenged Nuggins.

"The name is Breedlove. This bantam rooster by my side is known as Bowers. Don't be deceived by a stunted stature. We're friends of peace. Tonight we're upholding the legal duties of an administrator. Any objections?"

"You're playing a weak hand too strong," warned Nuggins. "We ain't asking the help of strangers. You'll get your whiskers singed."

At this particular point Indigo obeyed his instincts and changed front. Ever since he and Joe had ridden into the country he had been protesting that he wanted to be out of it. He had disliked Dead Card John from the moment he first laid eyes on the man. And with every step along the pathway of trouble he had angrily warned Joe he would bear no part in it; he didn't propose to help any renegade

110

steal a ranch. Yet when Praygood Nuggins challenged Joe, Indigo Bowers's scruples ceased to matter. Instantly he was aflame with hostility, instantly the washed-out eyes took on that greenish hue which was for this little man a sure and inevitable sign of fighting wrath.

Indigo was not a character to reflect or follow his reason. He was a bundle of nerves, a harbinger of grief and gloom, he was a repository of dynamite. Once feeling that his dignity had been infringed upon or his wisdom and courage questioned Indigo was full ready to fight the Angel Gabriel's heavenly warriors, nine wildcats and an entire room full of assorted badmen. And when he reached that pitch of temper he was fully capable of tearing down the premises, board by board; caution was not in him then and his hundred-odd pounds left a cyclonic trail of wreckage behind.

So he twisted his nose and tilted his small chin and stabbed Nuggins with a glittering glance. "Poor hands is our favored way of playing cards. Listen, you yellow-whiskered, frost-faced son of original sin, you're so crooked the sun can't cast a shadow behind you. A snake in the grass is a messenger of charity compared to a man what would steal a gal's ranch. Buy it, you said? Who in hell believes you'd ever pay a nickel? Your friend Al, which does all the dirty washing, tinkered with Mamerock's messenger to get invites. We saw that play in town. Your friend Al tinkered with this fellow Dead Card John's men. We saw that out by the road saloon. Your friend Al's been tinkering with Ox Bow men tonight at the bridge. And we saw that. Why, man, you ought to be a foreign diplomat you're so smooth. Don't tell us where to head in. Joe and me has cut our gums on jaspers like you."

All the while he had his thumbs hooked in his belt. And all the while Joe Breedlove was smiling in a tight, suppressed manner. The sheriff, Crowheart Ames, stepped away from the whisky barrels, roughly challenging Indigo. "Hey there! Pull in that crooked nose of yours. We'll do our own family fighting without help. You and your friend hit the Terese jail tomorrow. Chew on that. Now stand back and let white folks talk."

Indigo faced the sheriff, polite to the point of deadliness. "Yeah? My nose may be crooked, Mister Ames, but I ain't got a face that looks like a mush bowl turned wrong side out. What are you so proud of? I guess we could tell a few things about your recent history likewise. You been trading hosses in the middle of the stream lately and right now you don't know which side of this argument's going to come out clear and bring you your profit."

"Gospel," drawled Joe. "Indigo, you sure are wound up." He watched Praygood Nuggins, waiting for open aggressiveness; the latter seemed to be testing the tide.

But Crowheart Ames was thoroughly enraged. "By God, I'm tossing you two troublemakers in the root cellar now! Put up your hands!"

"Not for a while," interposed Joe softly. "I guess it's about time to set the ball rolling. Me and my partner are declaring ourselves. Come on, Indigo."

They circled the sheriff, never letting him out of sight, and stopped beside Dead Card John. "How's politics in this room?" Joe asked. "It don't make no difference to me what this gent's past history is. He's on the right side of the fence now. Who's declaring for him? He's upholding the girl, ain't he? Why not give him a ride, then? If he starts putting anything in his own pockets the county ought to be strong enough to haze him down when said time comes. As between the devil and the deep blue sea, I'll take to water myself. Nuggins, your hat hides your horns!"

Thunder rode Nuggins. "You've wrote your own ticket, friend! I never let a man interfere with my ideas!" He ducked his head around the room. "All right, boys. Come over here and line up."

The sheriff started to speak, but crowded the words back down his throat. For the tide drifted both ways. Nuggins collected some of the Ox Bow men to him, some of the visiting punchers, and a few of his own men who had managed to cross the bridge. The old-timers to a man stuck to their own group, beside the sheriff. What astonished Joe, and therefore possibly silenced Crowheart Ames, was the support Dead Card John pulled from the assemblage. Six Ox Bow men, the partners, the saloon proprietor from Terese, and a scattering of young bloods, these were with him. And after another moment, three of the old-timers left the neutral bunch with some show of reluctance and added to Dead Card John's strength. It did not match the strength of Nuggins by half, but it was sufficient to check any immediate rush.

"Every penny of this ranch and every inch of it goes to the girl," droned Dead Card John. "There's my word. You know I never go back on that, Nuggins."

"It may go to the girl," snapped Nuggins, "but it may come back to you again, John. You're both the same kind. The two of you ribbed old Rube!"

"Be careful, Nuggins!"

"I got you over a barrel, Johnny," cried Nuggins, using the words as he would have used a knife. They slashed

112

through the smoke-laden air. "It took me five years to sap you. I got you licked. This ranch is mine. I said so! I'll pay a figure out of the earnin's and no man in Terese can say it ain't legal. You ain't big enough any more to stand in my way, Johnny!"

"Be careful, Nuggins!"

Crowheart Ames's little eyes jumped from side to side. He took off his hat and pushed his fingers nervously across his hair, a plain picture of a thoroughly bedeviled man. The scene and the situation ran rapidly beyond control. Turning to the kegs he scooped another dipper of whisky into his bulldog jaws. Those old-timers in the neutral ranks were studying him with an uncomfortable closensss. One of them leaned and whispered in his ear. Crowheart's whole face lightened. "Yeah," he muttered. "Why didn't I think of it before?"

Nuggins launched his challenge to Dead Card John. "Take your men and get out! I give you two minutes to pass the doors. You're trespassing on my property."

"In two minutes," was Dead Card John's brief, chill answer, "we will draw guns."

The sheriff stepped between the parties. "No fight," he announced. "We've got to cool off and do some figuring. Nuggins, take your men out to the bunkhouses and wait. Me and these gentlemen—" pointing to the neutral bunch— "will collect at the barn and do some auguring."

"I'm not moving an inch," snapped Nuggins.

One of the neutral men challenged this. "No? How far do you think that's going to ride? You be reasonable. We want some time to compare notes. We ain't against you, Nuggins. But we'll just take control till we decide who's right."

Nuggins shook his head. "I'll share this house with Johnny."

"Johnny stays," replied the spokesman of the neutrals. "You go, plenty prompt. Don't get us sore. We got you outnumbered and if you're going to get pig-headed we're apt to throw in with the other side. Bustle."

The sheriff was watching Nuggins and his head dropped a faint distance in signal. Nuggins gave in. "All right. At the bunkhouses." Dead Card John and his followers held steady as Nuggins led his crowd into the rain-swept night. Crowheart Ames and the neutral ranchers followed.

"Close the door—lock it," said Dead Card John.

Joe stepped over and did it.

"Smells like more spoiled beef to me," grumbled Indigo. Joe raced across the room in great strides, shattering the globes of the reflecting lamps. A burst of shots smashed the front window panes. "Drop!" shouted Joe, and made a leap for the remaining lamp. They went down to the floor, the room in semi-darkness. The saloon proprietor from Terese groaned. "They took a tuck in my ribs, boys."

CHAPTER 5

"Roll away from the front of the fire," ordered Dead Card John.

Window glass elsewhere in the house splintered and jangled on the floor. "How many doors to this shebang?" demanded Joe, plastered in a corner.

"They're all locked," answered an Ox Bow man. "I seen to that a long time back. Hell, I thought them old dudes was Rube's friends. They's a pack of flea-bitten dawgs and they only got out of the house to save their rotten hides from bein' perforated."

One of the three ranch owners who had deserted from the neutral group challenged this with mild anger. "I don't take that kindly. Those gentlemen are friends of mine. Keep your heavy tongue off 'em. Ames is only waiting to see which side wins before declaring himself. They know it and they ain't being fooled none. But mebbe you think it's an easy job to figger this scramble?"

"It looks plain enough to me," said the Ox Bow man.

"Well, it don't to them. Don't you mistake it none, they'll fight. But they ain't helping nobody till they're plumb shore a ketch ain't involved."

Joe raised his gun and took aim into the night. A roar and a spattering of lead slugs filled the room. The driving wind found the apertures in the shattered glass and raced against the fireplace, fanning it to a white, tall blaze. A back door splintered and the partners, galloping toward that quarter at the head of six or so others, met Nuggins's men head-on. The door was off its hinges and the opening filled and spilling over. Some thoughtful defender shot out a light, leaving nothing to the sight save a square rectangle of uneasy blackness where the door had been. Gun flashes made purple-orange clusters there; a long, wild cry beat inward, flesh struck flesh. Impact and recoil. Powder smoke belched back, whipped by the wind. And the gun flashes faded and the sortie was ended, one man's groan of ebbing mortality marking the effort that had been made.

Dead Card John rallied them back to the main room.

"One fellow watch this opening. Rest at the other side of the house. I think they're trying to draw us off guard."

They assembled in the shadowed corners, waiting. One lone shot drummed along the rain. Boots shuffled across the floor. "Lights coming on in the bunkhouses. Guess they got a bellyful. Lights in the barn, too."

"Waiting for daylight," observed Indigo. "Which is help to them and no good use to us."

"Why not?" asked Dead Card John, somewhere in the remote shadows.

"A river which goes up can likewise come down," opined Indigo. "If ever they get the rest of their outfit across the water we'll be in bad shape. Not mentioning the fact and possibility of this Ames jasper swinging the old ducks his way. Proceeding with the inquest I will state we ain't got enough men to scatter 'round this castle and head off a daylight attack."

Somebody away back in the room vented his disgust. "You sound like an undertaker. If you got chilblains, clear out."

Joe interceded. He had a great respect for his partner's sense of strategy. Indigo could not plan ahead, neither was he a very good judge or leader of men. But once a situation hung in front of his nose he had no superior in picking the weak and the strong angles. This was born not of imagination but of long experience. Therefore, Joe came to Indigo's assistance. "You boys take note. Indigo's no specimen of beauty, but he's been in more arguments than the pack of you fellows put together. Right now he's talking sound."

"Yeah? Well, what about it?"

"Why wait for 'em to visit us?" proceeded Indigo. "Le's get four-five boys together and shoot a few holes in their doghouse. When you keep a man busy brushing lead off his shoulders he's plumb apt to get discouraged."

Silence met his proposal. Some rash individual crouched in front of the fire and proceeded to light a cigarette. "Don't do that!" snapped Dead Card John.

"What time is it?"

"Going on three in the morning. Couple hours till we can see something."

Indigo emitted a sound half between pain and anger. "Sa-ay, what am I smelling?"

"Grub, mister. They's a whole table full of beans yonder."

Indigo's boots echoed across the room and into the adjoining one like the clatter of cavalry troop. And they heard him murmuring, "Sometimes I sure do pass up a bet."

Dead Card John took command of the conversation. "About that idea of going out after them. It's a good one. Any volunteers?"

"How about yourself?" queried some slightly suspicious individual.

"Never ask a man to do anything I wouldn't try first," was Dead Card John's ice-cold reply. "And I will kindly beg you to remember you are not fighting for me but for the girl." His voice rose to a higher, incredibly bitter note. "I would see you all in hell before I'd ask a favor on my own account! Who's got nerve enough to tackle the bunkhouse?"

That touched them. Out of the screening darkness they cursed him; they were rising up to the challenge. But Joe Breedlove had another idea and another purpose. "Wait a second. Before you get started on this bust, I want to crawl over to the barn and see what that collection of whiskers has got figured out."

"Another good idea."

Joe aimed for the door Nuggins's outfit had battered down. "Back in a little while. If I ain't, draw your own conclusions."

"Hey," shouted Indigo, sounding strangled. "Wait till I find the bottom of this bean crock."

"No, you stay put," decided Joe, and bent his head through the whirling gusts of rain.

He cleared the door at one long jump, landed on his haunches and crouched there, waiting. Nothing happened. Rising, he turned directly toward the lights glimmering out of the barn apertures. Against the lee shelter of its walls, he waited again, one ear tight against the boards. But the wind and the rain, still slanting furiously from the sky drowned all other sound and he turned a corner and bore down upon the front entrance. The great sliding door was closed, the lesser door cut within it rattled to the pressure of his shoulder. He lifted the latch and crowded through, lantern light springing upon him. The neutrals were slouched in the straw; Crowheart Ames sat cross-legged behind the lantern's golden glow, heavy lids squinting up and across the bowl of radiance. "Who's that?"

"One of the strangers."

The sheriff sprang to his feet. "I'll take care of him right now!"

Joe came forward and squatted within the circle, conscious that this group watched him with the same curious closeness that a hunting pack would bestow upon a treed coon. The sheriff started to cross the center of the group and was stopped by an admonitory hand. "Sit down, Crow-heart. It ain't your party, is it?"

Joe made note of the speaker. He had seen the man talk-ing confidentially to Mamerock earlier in the evening. He had heard a name—something like Bristow—attached to him by Mamerock. And this Bristow at present seemed a leader of the gathering; a chap with coal-black whiskers and coal-black eyes. He flashed them on Joe Breedlove. "What's on your mind, brother?"

Breedlove eased himself nearer the light, relaxing; and he smiled that frank, disarming smile that never yet had failed to win him friends and followers. His palms turned up, Indian fashion; he looked around the circle and back into the tiers of men half hidden outside the ring of light, glance returning to meet Bristow's straight, blunt regard.

"Wondered if you fellows had reached a decision yet."

"Dead Card John send you?"

"It's my own curiosity," replied Joe. "But I'd say the other boys are some interested."

Bristow shot a quick question at him, reminding Joe of a prosecuting attorney he once had faced long ago. "What profit do you get hauling Dead Card John's chestnuts out of the fire, stranger?"

Joe smiled once more. "I'm a hell of a fellow to mind my own business, till something stings me." The smile vanished. "My partner and I saw Sam Trago dead up in his folks' house. We overheard a lot of things since. We got a ticket to Rube Mamerock's fandango. I might ask you the same question, friend. Why should you pull Nuggins's chestnuts out of the fire?"

"Who says we are?"

"Write your own ticket. Here you boys augur, while said gent plants a bunch of lead into the house. Looks to me as if you wanted Nuggins to steal the girl's right."

"Don't get so previous about it," grunted Bristow. He leaned back, frowning into the straw. "Maybe you think we ain't been debating it a little. Seems to me that for a mature, shrewd-looking man you take a lot of stock in Dead Card John. Don't you know a crook when you see one?"

"Which likewise applies to Nuggins," countered Joe mildly.

"Yeah, we know that better'n you do," muttered Bristow.

Crowheart Ames leaned into the light, florid and threat-ening. "You talk too damn' much for a stranger! Dead Card John ribbed old Mamerock some way. It's as plain as the nose on your face. Mamerock spent most of his life cussing folks like Johnny. It don't stand to reason he'd change in a minute."

Joe looked at Bristow. The latter nodded, confirming that idea. "It's the way we look at it, stranger."

Joe got out his cigarette papers, and talked casually, half to himself. "So Terese lets the girl fight her own battles. Well, I've heard of people like that—"

"Hell's pit!" exploded Bristow. "Who said we aimed to let her lose her rights? But we ain't playing Dead Card John's cards for him, either."

"Then you play Nuggins's," said Joe with unmistakable definiteness.

"Nuggins can be hazed into line," argued Bristow, "if he tries anything funny."

"Why argue with this jasper?" stormed the sheriff. "We don't owe him no apologies. Great Moses, you gents aggravate me! He'd ought to be in jail or rid out on a rail. I'm going to see it done before this is through."

Joe went serenely on with the business of manufacturing his cigarette. Nothing disturbed the even set of his face, yet his mind raced down long alleys of thought. He felt the uncertainty of these neutrals. They were between two fires, reluctant to throw in with a notorious character, yet desiring to see the will of an ancient friend carried out. Another thing he knew: these men had a trace of fear when it came to Nuggins. The latter was a power, a sinister influence, while Dead Card John's star was setting. And it was because of all this that Bristow, mirroring the thought of the crowd, unconsciously put himself on the defensive to a complete stranger. Joe crimped his cigarette and lit it.

"I've always found it never pays to be scared of any man. Always found said man could be knocked over somehow. It only takes one bullet to kill Nuggins's kind."

The shot was shrewdly aimed. He heard the rumbling rise of protest all around him. It had touched them on a sore spot. Bristow's intensely black eyes filled with a hot, personal anger. "I don't take that kindly, stranger. Who are you to tell folks they're yellow?"

"Ain't I told you it's time to knock him over?" cried Crowheart Ames, weaving forward.

But this crowd was not to be swayed by the sheriff. Somebody to the rear of Joe cursed Ames and told him to hold his peace. Crowheart's unlovely face dropped; he sat on his haunches, perplexed and uneasy.

"If," drawled Joe, never raising his voice, "you boys

knew this Dead Card John meant what he said about protecting the girl's rights would it help any?"

He heard a note of encouragement in the rumbling comment. Bristow's black beard bobbed in acknowledgment. "That'd be the end of talk, then and there," said he. "But nobody believes what he says. It ain't in the cards. The man's played Terese for his own gains a long time, stranger. And I told you once we ain't helping his hand none."

"What was the girl's name?" asked Joe, seeming to wander off in his mind.

"Chasteen."

Joe drew a deep breath of smoke. He knew well that if what he was about to say was to carry conviction he must first convince them of his own honesty. And he could only do that by keeping his mouth shut and letting them look at him. All his credentials were on his face; no word would help. So he straightened, a tall, soldierly and sinewy outline with the yellow light stamping the fine, rugged features. He was in the full vigor of his maturity, he had seen the West inside and out down along the far trail of his roaming. And because Joe had been hurt badly, because he had fought bravely, he could stand before this crowd now and impress them with the gentle, honest tolerance that was so great a part of his character. He had swayed men before, he did it now. And the very lifting of his cigarette brought a deeper silence to the barn.

"I guess I've been a drifting fool all my life," he drawled. "When a man sleeps under the stars enough times a house won't do. And when he follows the trail so many miles, a steady job can't hold him. I'm the sort of a man you gents hire for a season and never see again. West is full of 'em. I never knew my folks. Started on the spur when I was fourteen. A long time ago. Once in Abilene—"

The great barn door surged to the wind, the lantern guttered. Bristow put a vast hand around the globe top. Crowheart Ames watched Joe out of the shadows. Somebody smothered a cough.

"—Once in Abilene, fifteen years ago, I blew in with money burning holes in my jeans. And I sat up to a poker game and lost it. I remember it most clearly because a woman sang through that crowd like I never heard anybody sing since. And she was toting a little girl in her arms while she sang. Through that rough crowd—singing the kid to sleep while she sang for the house. And I remember her looking at the professional which was relieving me and four others of our spare cash. A woman only looks at one man like that. Then she passes on, singing down the lanes. I'm reading my cards close and I makes a bet, but the professional don't seem to hear me. He's pretty young, too, and as handsome as a marble statue. You know. But he's looking after the woman. Some kind of a word passes 'round that saloon. I turns and sees her close to some other gent. She'd stopped singing and was talking to him. Next I knew the hair was singed on the top of my head, I hears the woman screaming, and since then I never have been able to stand the sound. But the fellow near her is on the floor and the gambler at my table is going hell-bent for the door. Never saw him in Abilene again."

He lifted the cigarette, turning it in his fingers so that small spirals of smoke jetted upward. He inclined forward just a little and each following word dropped rhythmically into the silence. "I want to tell you boys, Dead Card John will see that girl gets every penny of her will. How long's he been in the country—five-ten years? Yeah. And he ain't ever told a soul his name, and he ain't ever made friends with man, woman or child. He's a crook, always was a crook. But I'm telling you he'll keep his word tonight and tomorrow and the next day to that girl. For his real name is Chasteen, and he was the gambler I sat with a long time back in Abilene. And this Ray Chasteen, though she don't know it, is his own daughter."

"Get out! Wait—here, figure this. Ray's mama, Jenny Chasteen, died here six years back. No, five. Dead Card John drifted in right after. Ray was took care of by folks in Terese. She's been singing going on four years, like her mama. I've seen Dead Card John stand by the bar and listen—" Bristow stopped and reared, black eyes snapping. "But I don't believe it none!"

"Who picked the girl out of the sheriff's arms last night when she fainted in the saloon?" was Joe's gentle interrogation.

"Hell's pit! But, man, why wouldn't he say he was her dad—if he was?"

Joe shook his head, wistfully sad. "The man's been a crook all his life. He shot a gent in Abilene out of plain jealousy. And then he run, deserting a wife and little girl. Do you figure he'd tell her now? She's straight, she was to be married to a straight gent. No, it was Dead Card John's play to keep his mouth shut and feed on his heart because of what he couldn't do. I'm telling a man's secret, which I'd ought to be shot for. But that's why I'm on his side of the fence."

Bristow got up and looked around at his friends. "Well, boys?"

They were all on their feet, crowding down into the light. Crowheart Ames spread his elbows to keep his place, protesting. "Say, don't swallow that guff. What're you going to do?"

"Shut up, Ames!"

Somebody spoke quietly and swiftly to Bristow. "Get that bunch out of the ranch house. We'll set a ring around Nuggins's party and take him to camp."

"Done."

"I'll bring the boys this far," said Joe, turning to the door. "Turn out the lantern. If I was you, I'd hold Mister Ames close by. When Nuggins loses, Mister Ames also loses a cut in the profits." He bent into the sweeping rain with the sound of the sheriff's struggle behind; he crossed to the main house, challenged the open door softly and passed the guard. Somebody collided with him; Indigo cursed the blackness. "Get off my bunions, you clodhopper."

"All right, let's travel."

"Oh—Joe?"

Dead Card John answered from near the fireplace. "What are they doing?"

Joe smiled. And being a wise man, he was glad he could say this in the darkness. "I just got 'em in good humor by reciting a few stories about when I was a kid in Abilene. Upon mature judgment the old-timers figured they'd play our cards. They'll be waiting by the barn. Let's go."

Above the scraping of feet and the clash of voice he heard Dead Card John's reply, even and threatening. "I want to see you at daylight, Breedlove."

"Daylight's an hour off," murmured Joe, "and lots of water will run under the bridge meanwhile." Indigo was beside him, identified by a honeyed, singsong profanity. Shoulder to shoulder they left the ranch house and slid across the muddy yard. They were challenged at the barn, the groups merged.

Bristow assumed command with a crisp order. "You fellows spread around the bunkhouses to the right. We'll take the left and do the same. I'll give Nuggins a chance to come out with a whole skin and no trouble. If they figure to argue the matter, let 'em have it in the guts."

The partners turned and started circling the lights of the bunkhouse. Bristow's cautious summons came faintly through the sheeting rain. "Where's that tall stranger? I want him with me."

Joe swung back, pulling Indigo with him. "A grandstand seat for us."

"It don't feel right to me," grumbled Indigo. "This Nuggins is a man who wouldn't expose himself in a place like that, with lights burning. They's a dead skunk in the barnyard."

They found Bristow by his repeated summons. Indigo, as wary as a wolverine, wanted to know where the sheriff was.

"One of my men was watching him last I knew," said Bristow.

"I'll bet he's shed his skin and departed elsewhere," Indigo prophesied. "That bunkhouse light burns plumb too steady."

"Come on. We'll find out in a minute."

The crowd had melted away. Bristow and the partners, accompanied by a fourth man unknown to Joe, walked directly toward the light, side by side. Figures cut across the beacon's outflung beams—Bristow's party running around the place. Twenty yards from it, the four stopped.

"I'll go and kick open the door," said Joe. "And step aside. You fellows do the necessary talking."

He left them, touched the bunkhouse wall and crawled along it until his exploring fingers reached the latch. He wasted no time; up came the latch. His boot struck the door and threw it open. Recoiling in the shadows, he heard Bristow, somewhere to one side of the wide and yellow beam, shout a harsh command. "You're surrounded. We got you two to one, Nuggins! Come out and give up— By God, they've flew the coop!"

"Hah!" yelled Indigo, "I thought so! That sheriff jasper— lookit the barn!"

A gun exploded twice over by the ranch house. Joe knew then Nuggins had swapped shelter and now held the fort. Turning at Indigo's command, he saw the barn emitting a blood-red glow. It grew with incredible swiftness; a tongue of flame lashed out of a loft opening, the windows were like ruby eyes. All that straw and loose hay seemed to catch at once and to set up a small explosion that tore the great door from its runway; the shadows of the yard were dissolved.

"Under the spot!" yelled Indigo. "Now ain't that fine! Come on—we're targets right now! Tear that damn' house off its foundations!"

Joe galloped over the slippery earth to come abreast of his enraged, embattled partner. The rest of the besiegers closed upon the house in a long and irregular line. Indigo, whose every instinct was fashioned for a moment like this, launched a shrill yell at them. "Buck into it—tackle it all sides. Some of you buzzards flap your wings up the porch posts. Keep 'm busy—bust the windows—ram down the front door. Eeeyip! I never did like this mess, but I aim to get my money's worth now."

The barn walls were sho. with red streaks; the tinder-dry rafters inside began to snap and crash. There was a vast droning of air rushing through the open mouth of the place and a snoring of flames high against the roof. That sharp snapping sounded a great deal like gunshots to Joe; and when a jet of mud sprang out of the ground and plastered his cheeks he understood his ears hadn't been playing him tricks. Nuggins had his men posted at every available aperture on this side of the house. One of the party beside him weaved like a drunk and pitched headlong in the muck, rolling over and over. Joe and Indigo and Bristow arrived at the caved-in rear door of the house at the same moment and threw themselves out of range. Flat in the mud they felt the sudden explosion inside. The trap had sprung before the quarry entered its jaws.

"Now," grunted Joe. All three of them hooked their guns around the side posts and raked the interior. Diversion. "Now," repeated Joe. The three rose and plunged inside, broke apart and hurled themselves onward across the floor. Fom the corner of his eye, Joe saw Indigo bent far over, feet planted wide, throwing shot after shot into some black corner. The little man was at the peak of his fighting capacity. But Bristow had either fallen or gone on into the main room. As for himself Joe rammed a table and felt his feet come from under him, locked around by a pair of arms. In falling, he turned and doubled. His gun laid along solid flesh, the grip on his legs relaxed; his third twist brought him across the man's body and he smashed his gun barrel a second time upon the other. That fight was over. Joe ripped the assailant's revolver free and crawled out to open space.

The blazing barn sent its light into the house through every opening. Light and shadow laid side by side. Men ran all over the place; they stamped across the floor above him, they fought solitary duels from room to room. Somebody rolled down the stairway, taking a part of the railing with him. Indigo's shrill cry sounded out of a remote corner and Joe, wiping blood from his nose, knew that nothing but wreckage lay along his partner's trail. As for himself, he got up and hurried into the main room.

The house was crowded with attacker and attacked and the semi-darkness was all in favor of Nuggins's smaller party. He ran to the fireplace, kicking the logs to fresh flame. He circled the walls, striking a match at each wick. A shot splintered the floor at his feet; whirling, he swept the corners, and saw nothing. Either the shot was a stray or else somebody hung around a corner, out of sight. Somehow, the fighters avoided this main room. They were advancing and retreating to distant crooks and crannies.

Joe edged toward the front of the room, attention divided between two possible coverts. The door leading into the dining room struck him as being open to inspection and he trained his gun upon it, walking in an arc that would give him a better view. Somebody shouted. Crowheart Ames plunged through that door, hatless, wild-eyed.

"Where they at? Where's Dead Card Johnny—Nuggins?"

Joe studied the man narrowly. It seemed to him this precipitous entrance had been badly faked. "What side are you fighting on, Mister Ames?"

The sheriff dropped his gun, glowering at Joe. "It ain't my place to do no fighting. If I plug a few shots at Nuggins it's all right because he's in wrong. But it don't help a law officer none to get tangled in a private war. I'm out of it right now."

"Still playing both ends against the middle, Mister Ames?"

"You know too much!" cried the sheriff. "I'd advise you to keep your mouth shut. It'll pay you. This is a big county to get lost in."

"Next time you want to take a pot shot at me," said Joe, "get a little farther away or I'll drop you."

The echo of fighting grew smaller. Men were collecting in adjoining rooms, checking up. There was a scuffle upstairs and an exchange of shots out in the yard. Joe heard a faint sound come through the door beside the fireplace, in that room whence Rube Mamerock had taken the girl earlier in the evening. He stepped over and threw the door open. Crowheart Ames drew a great breath, as if to shout. Joe turned and checked it with a single glance. A lamp sat on a table of that room and two men stood face to face across the light—Dead Card John and Praygood Nuggins, each with his hands clamped against the table's edge, each bending forward.

"Shut the door, please," droned Dead Card John, never moving his eyes.

Joe quietly closed it. Crowheart Ames looked around him wildly and Joe saw the sudden sweat breaking through the sheriff's fat jowls. Men came down the stairs and in from the night and out of the dining room. Nuggins's partisans had been corralled, beaten and bereft of their weapons. Bristow appeared from the outside, soaking wet. And he looked to Joe.

"Where's Dead Card John?"

Joe inclined his head toward the back room. Bristow started toward it, but stopped at Joe's warning shake of his head. "Nuggins is there also."

The sheriff began to swear. "I ain't goin' to stand here—" His whole body shook. Two shots exploded behind the door, a splinter rose from the paneling; and then the crowd, dead still, heard one more shot. But there was no other hole in the paneling. Boots struck the door, it opened; Dead Card John walked out, eyes brilliant against his white skin.

"The gentleman is dead."

Bristow nodded as if it were a matter of course, and not particularly important. He began checking over the prisoners. "You boys have caused a hell of a mess. Maybe you had an honest doubt about Rube's will. I'd be the last man to hold that against you. But when you knew we old-timers decided to throw in with Dead Card John, you ought to've had sense enough to figure the fight was over. You didn't. You spilled blood. You played with Nuggins, knowing damn' well what Nuggins aimed to do. All right. Now you're all going to the jug and let Terese County think about it. Ames—rope these fellows up and watch 'em!"

The sheriff rose. "Listen—"

Bristow exploded. "By Judas, don't stand there and argue! You're skating on thin ice right now. We got a mind to bust you. Do as you're told and do it sudden."

Ames said nothing more. His forefinger tolled off a few men to help him. A man, quicker minded than the others, appeared from the night with a bunch of ropes and tossed them to willing hands. Bristow looked thoughtfully at Joe, seeming to debate over a particularly hard question.

"Where's the girl?"

"Upstairs," said a puncher.

Bristow turned and went up.

Indigo limped in from outside, water pouring out of him at every step. The fighting fervor was gone and he looked like some bantam rooster that had been doused with the water bucket. Gloom wreathed itself on his thin cheeks. He was a figure of suspicion and despair. And without a word he passed into the dining room and began occupying himself with a crock of beans. Joe started to follow, then swung back with narrowing eyes. Ames returned from his trip, holding a rifle in his hands.

"Where did you steal that, Mister Ames?"

The sheriff had been beaten badly and there was nothing but sullen resentment in him. "I'll take no lip off you, stranger. It's my own rifle."

"Yeah?" drawled Joe. "What kind of a rifle? Looks like I saw somebody else using that tonight."

The sheriff refused to answer. An adjoining puncher spoke for him. "It's his gun, all right, stranger. Nobody but him has got a Krag."

Joe squared his shoulders, the pleasantry fading from his blue eyes. The crowd, puzzled by the scene, gave Joe a curious attention. Indigo heard his partner talking and, from the tone Joe used, he knew trouble to be in the air. Spurning the bean crock he crossed to his partner's side.

Joe pointed at the sheriff's gun. "He says it's his gun, and that he's always owned it. I been furnished with the further information that he's about the only gent around Terese using a Krag."

"What about it?" growled Ames, frowning. He was angry and nervous and ill at ease.

Joe put thumb and forefinger in his vest pocket. "Maybe that explains a mystery I figured wouldn't ever come to light. Me and my partner was up at Sam Trago's shanty yesterday and we ran across the spot where he'd been ambushed. And we found this shell." He pulled it out and held it up for inspection. And he added, very quietly, "It's a Krag shell."

It was a tribute to Joe's power that, as he threw the shell to the floor, no single man stooped to verify it. Dead Card John jumped away from the fireplace, reaching for his armpit.

"Stop that!" warned Joe, and put himself between the man and Ames.

Ames dropped the rifle; his arm fell to his gun and ripped upward. The crowd stood rooted, failing to catch the speed of the play. But Joe was smiling in the face of the sheriff's revolver; smiling with his lips pressed together and his blue eyes flickering queerly. He had matched the sheriff's draw. So they stood, deadlocked and a bare three yards apart. Ames had taken a step backward, putting himself clear of the crowd.

"You been wanting action, stranger," he shouted. "Now come and get it! Terese ain't big enough for you and me. You lie about that shell. I never was near Trago's shanty that day."

"Another lie!" broke in Dead Card John coldly.

"I been wanting to know what the state of your nerve was," mused Joe. "Ever since I saw you in the saloon, I been wanting to know it. Ames, you're yellow. Go on and

126

pull the trigger. Take a chance. Stand up there—don't get a kink in your back!"

"It's your last play," muttered Ames. His grotesque face was warped, the chin so far forward that the upper lip dropped down upon the nether teeth. Sweat trickled down the far curve of his cheeks and made a glistening pool in the blue stubble on his chin.

"What's the matter with your back? Starch all gone out of it? I'm counting five, Ames. If your gun don't drop by then—one, and two, and three—"

Ames's arm fell swiftly. A weird and strangled yell left his throat; turning, he clawed for the door. At that the crowd broke and in the ensuing jam Joe saw the sheriff go down. He holstered his weapon, sighing as if he were tired.

"I wasn't so doggoned sure about him being yellow," he murmured. "But he'll hang."

Bristow came down the stairway with Ray Chasteen. And when Joe saw her looking toward Dead Card John, he retreated into the dining room, pulling Indigo after him. "What's the matter now?" grumbled the small partner.

Joe shook his head, taking a final glance at the scene. The girl ran across the room and threw her arms around Dead Card John; and he heard her say, "Dad!" He shook his head, swearing softly at his weariness, and when he looked again he found Dead Card John nothing more than a man, after all. Dead Card John was crying.

"Come away, Indigo. The party's over. Rube put on a good fandango. He'd sure be pleased to know how much of a success it was. Come on, Indigo."

"What the hell—out in the rain again?"

"He said he wanted to see me at daylight," replied Joe, ducking through the rear door. "But I'm running away from him. Don't want to see him. It's daylight, ain't it?"

The barn was a red skeleton that illumined all the island. Gray dawn broke along the sullen eastern rim. And the rain came down steadily. They got their horses out of the shed —whence the animals had drifted since last used—and turned past the barn and bunkhouse toward the east end of the island.

"You can't cross this water," objected Indigo.

"Got to. Indigo, I'd rather drown than meet Dead Card John. Yeah, I would. I don't look so bad by light. Let's try the old channel. I see a trail up the bluff, once we ford the water."

"It don't make no difference to me. I'm as wet as I ever could be. There's a shallow spot."

They stood a moment on the edge, watching the current

curling over the gravel. At best, it was a difficult crossing even with the firelight of the barn to guide them. Joe urged his horse into it and kicked his feet out of the stirrups. Twenty minutes later the two of them poised on the bluff and looked back, downward upon the Ox Bow. They saw men moving restlessly around the yard; they heard a gun's report.

"Looking for us, I bet," said Indigo. "What makes you so afraid of meeting that jasper?"

"Bristow told her what I told him. Dead Card John is her daddy. Met him in Abilene once. She'll forgive him. No matter how bad he's been she'll forgive him. And don't you think he won't run that outfit smooth. The man's had his punishment. It wouldn't be in a woman's heart to quit him now."

"Well, what're you afraid of then?"

Joe smiled. "He wanted to kill me once for telling. Right now I reckon he wants to thank me. He ain't a man that's had much practice in showing gratitude. He'd make a terrible botch of it, Indigo. So we're relieving him of the trouble."

Indigo swore a while. They turned east again and rode toward Terese. The gray morning dawned. Joe shook his head. "Indigo, it's winter. We've got to figure about holing up."

"Yeah," said Indigo, not meeting his partner's eyes. "Tell you what. We'll eat and take a wink in Terese. Then we'll ride south and think on it with some mature judgment. And we'll finally decide what to do when we get to the next sizable town."

"Agreed."

Indigo muttered something to himself. He had seen a map of the country the previous night and he knew what Joe didn't yet know. The next sizable town south of Terese was a full hundred miles. That was staving off difficulty for quite a few days.

So, silently, they jogged toward Terese in the driving rain.

THE END